THE SONG OF ORPHEUS:
THE GREATEST GREEK MYTHS
YOU NEVER HEARD

ALSO BY TRACY BARRETT

Anna of Byzantium

On Etruscan Time

The Sherlock Files:
    Book 1: *The 100-Year-Old Secret*
    Book 2: *The Beast of Blackslope*
    Book 3: *The Case that Time Forgot*
    Book 4: *The Missing Heir*

King of Ithaka

Dark of the Moon

The Ancient Greek World (with Jennifer Roberts)

For more books and more information, see Tracy
Barrett's web site. To contact the author, go to:

http://www.tracybarrett.com/contact.htm

THE SONG OF ORPHEUS:
THE GREATEST GREEK MYTHS YOU NEVER HEARD

by
TRACY BARRETT

CONTENTS

INTRODUCTION

The Minotaur. Jason and the Argonauts. The goddess Athena springing full-grown from her father's head. King Midas and the golden touch. Arachne turning into a spider. Pandora's box.

Most fans of Greek mythology are familiar with some (or maybe all) of these stories. But even if you've heard of the one-eyed giant known as the Cyclops, you may not know about the bronze giant, Talos, who protected the island of Crete. You might recognize the three-headed dog, Cerberus, but are you familiar with the huge and uncatchable Teumessian Fox? Have you read about the mischievous Akmon and Passalos, who messed with the wrong superhero? What about the tragic tale of the sea goddess Leukothea, or the story of Tylos, who came back to life after being mauled to death by a dragon?

These names are probably unfamiliar even to people who have read a lot of Greek myths. That's because while the Greeks told many, many myths, worshipped many, many gods, and believed in many, many monsters and hybrid creatures and odd humans, the same dozen or so myths have been told and retold, while many others are practically unknown today.

Why? Some of the myths contradict each other, and in most of those cases, the less popular one has dropped out of sight. Others don't make much sense to modern people (and it seems they sometimes didn't make much sense to the ancient Greeks, either), so people stopped telling them. Some have the same plot with different names: god falls in love with girl, girl runs away from god, girl turns into a tree/stone/river, god is sad; or there's a prediction that a child will grow up to do something harmful, child is left outside to die, child survives with the help of an animal/shepherd/maid, child fulfills prophecy. People who publish mythology collections usually include only their favorite version of a myth.

Occasionally, an ancient writer drops a tantalizing hint about a myth we've never heard of—just enough to get a modern reader interested—but then nobody can find another trace of it. Scholars know that many myths the ancient Greeks used to share have been lost. Many myths were told aloud for centuries before anyone wrote them down, and most likely a lot of them never made it into written form. If they did get written down, the paper (or papyrus or parchment) might not have lasted long enough for modern people to be able to read what was on it.

But luckily, a lot of the less familiar myths *have* survived. Writings from the ancient world turn up in all sorts of places. Some have been found accidentally, bound up in a book along with a totally different text. Ancient writings have even been discovered on pieces of linen the Egyptians used to wrap their mummies in! It's very possible that still more writings will be discovered as more mummies are found and examined. If we're lucky, the archaeologists will find unfamiliar myths among them.

Where else might "new" myths be hiding? One possibility is in a bunch of what look like seriously overcooked dinner rolls. These are scrolls—rolled-up books that people in Europe used before they started making books with separate pages—that were scorched in the year 79 CE, when the volcano Vesuvius erupted and destroyed the cities of

Pompeii and Herculaneum, in southern Italy. The burnt scrolls found among the ruins of these cities can't be unrolled without crumbling into pieces, but scientists are working on finding a way to read them. Who knows? If they figure that out, maybe they'll find some new myths on those scrolls!

While everyone waits for new myths to be uncovered, here are some that have been preserved but, for one reason or another, have been left out of most anthologies. They're just as interesting as the ones that are told over and over again, but some may be unfamiliar to even the biggest fans of Greek mythology. In these stories are heroes to admire, clever solutions to tricky problems, sad love, happy love, new ways of looking at life, and surprise endings. A few may seem familiar at first but then take an unexpected turn. Others are wonderfully strange and puzzling. All of them deserve to be better known.

PROLOGUE
THE TALKING ROCK

You're in the middle of a dark wood, not sure how you got there or even exactly where you are. You must have wandered off the path when you weren't paying attention. For all you know, you could be in a thick forest that goes on and on for miles, or you could just as easily be in a corner of a small city park. Oddly, you don't feel afraid, but you are curious. You stop and listen, but you hear nothing except birdsong and the chatter of two squirrels spiraling up a tree. Then you catch the faint tinkle of running water, and you see light glinting off a creek just a few feet away.

Near the creek lies a rock. It's not very big—about the size of a bowling ball—but you notice it because it's all by itself, and also because of something strange: Twin streams of water are trickling out of two small dents in its surface. It's mossy and weathered, as though it's lain out here for a long, long time.

Then out of nowhere, you hear a voice. A man's voice.

Thank the gods you've come!

Oh, sorry to startle you. Don't you see me? There's no use looking for me over there. No, not up there, either. Look down. See me now? I'm that big rock by the stream, with water dripping down me. I know the water looks like tears, but I assure you, I'm not crying. It's just condensation from the dampness in this forest.

Why don't you come closer? It's not like I'm going to hurt you, for Zeus's sake. I can't grab you or run at you or anything. When did you last see a rock move, except in an earthquake or when someone pushed it down a hill? Or *up* a hill, the way that fool Sisyphus does, but his story isn't one I feel like telling. I can't move, I assure you. But as you've noticed, I can talk.

I suppose you're wondering how a rock can talk. It would be better if you wondered *why* a rock is talking.

Well, usually I *don't* talk. I sing. Would you like to hear me sing? Don't worry; even though I'm only a rock now, I have a lovely voice. The loveliest voice a mortal man ever possessed. My name is Orpheus. Have you ever heard of me?

No? Let me fill you in. I'm a musician, and I'm what you people nowadays call an "ancient Greek." My father was a king and my mother was a Muse—one of the famous nine Muses, in fact. The Muses, in case you didn't know, are goddesses who are in charge of music and dance and poetry and things like that.

I had a lot of adventures growing up, like meeting the god of music, Apollo. He gave me a lyre—a stringed instrument that isn't very popular anymore—and everyone said I played it better than anyone else who ever lived. I'm not bragging, just telling you what everyone said. I also went on a long sea voyage on a ship called the *Argo*, and more than once, I saved my companions' lives and my own with my singing.

I saw that look. You don't get how singing can save a life, right? Well, let me tell you, the songs and stories I sang were pretty powerful. In fact, it was my great voice that allowed me to do something that hardly anyone has ever done: I went to the land of the dead and returned alive. *Ah, that* surprises you! And it should. Like I said, hardly anyone has come back alive from the land of the dead. Only one person managed it before me—a big guy named Gilgamesh—and a few went there after me: a Trojan prince named Aeneas, then another Greek named Odysseus, though he didn't get very far before he got scared and came back out. A long time later, a Roman poet named Virgil dropped in with a gloomy Italian friend of his named Dante. There have been a few others over the centuries, but I'm the only one who's gone to the dark realm of the dead, while still living, for love.

Don't roll your eyes like that. Love is even more powerful than songs and stories—although come to think of it, most songs and stories seem to be about love, don't they? Anyhow, the way it happened was that I married a very nice girl named Eurydice and everything looked great until she got bitten by a snake and died on our wedding day. I know—pretty tragic, right? I was so upset that I went down into the realm of the dead and begged the king and queen to let me bring her back. They were all like no, you can't do that, dead is dead; but once I took out my lyre and sang a song about how sad I was, they cried and said all right. They said I could lead her out, but if I checked to see if she was behind me, they'd take her back again, this time for good. If I looked back, you see, that would mean I didn't trust their word. That would be an insult, and they didn't want to do any favors for someone who insulted them.

So I agreed to their terms and headed out, still singing. But I kept wondering whether Eurydice really was behind me. I stopped singing and listened, but I didn't hear any footsteps except my own. I stopped walking to make sure. Still nothing.

I couldn't stand it, so I thought I'd take such a quick look, barely turning my head, that nobody would notice.

The king and queen hadn't followed me, so how would they know if I just glanced over my shoulder?

I should have known better. The king and queen of the dead are gods, after all, and they can see what's going on in their entire kingdom, even in the places where they aren't. When I looked back, I saw my darling bride, Eurydice, disappearing before my eyes. She was being hauled back to the realm of the dead, crying and reaching out for me.

Well, I lost it. I called her name and tried to run after her, but I got confused in the shadows, with all the twists and turns. I wandered for a long time in the darkness before I finally came out on earth again, somewhere near here, wherever this is. I knew that the gods of the underworld wouldn't let me back into their realm, so I just roamed around, crying, until I accidentally stumbled into a party that some nymphs were having.

You don't know nymphs? They're kind of like girls, or women, but they're not really human and they're pretty wild. This party was supposed to be just for females, and when they saw me they were furious that a man had crashed it, and they leaped on me. I was so startled, I stopped singing, so I couldn't charm them the way I had the king and queen of the underworld. And the nymphs were *really* mad—crazy, even. And what they did.... Well, it's pretty bad. You sure you want to hear it?

Okay. They tore me to pieces, right there, and if you think it didn't hurt, you need to think harder. So you'd assume I would die, right, since I wasn't attached together anymore? No. That would have meant I'd go straight to the realm of the dead and be reunited with Eurydice, and the king and queen were still too angry with me to let that happen. So instead, they kept me alive while the nymphs scattered my body around. Then they turned my head into a rock and left me here by this stream.

There's only one way I can turn back into a human being. Oh, I won't be alive—nobody can live three thousand years, and when the sun sets tonight, it will be three thousand years since I was torn apart and then cursed with this rock head. But it will be a pleasure to die if I can just get out of here and finally be reunited with Eurydice. This is what I have to do: I have to tell three hundred stories within three thousand years. The catch is that they have to be stories that the other person has never heard before.

You'd think it would be easy, telling just three hundred stories in three thousand years, and at first, I figured I'd be out of here in a few months. But not many people come around this deep in the forest, and most of the ones who do get a little nervous when I start talking and they don't see anyone, so they don't stick around. And some of the ones who do stay have already heard a lot of my tales.

So I've only managed to tell 2,983 stories. Actually, 2,984, if you count me telling you how I got here, but I think it would be cheating to count that one. This time I'm going to be extra careful to play by the rules. So seventeen more to go.

What do you say? Want to hear a story? How about seventeen stories? If I tell them to you before the sun goes down, I'll be free. If not—well, I hate to think about it, but I imagine the gods will leave me here forever, and I just couldn't stand that. I'm tired of freezing in the winter and baking in the summer, and the bird poop alone is enough to make me sick of all this. Plus, I miss my wife, and I at least want the chance to apologize to her for being such a bonehead.

You will? You'll stay until I tell you seventeen stories you've never heard? Great! Let's start at the beginning—or rather, before the beginning.

BEFORE THE BEGINNING:
THE BIG BANG, GREEK-STYLE

I hear that nowadays Greece is a single country, but in my time, what is now the Greek nation was a bunch of small city-states. The people in the different city-states had different customs and they told different stories about the world, including how the world itself and the stars and planets came to be.

According to one of the stories, before humans walked the earth—before there even was an earth to walk on—before the gods ruled from Mount Olympos, or the stars shone in the sky, or there was light or air or even time, all that existed was Chaos (or Χάος, in Greek).

Now, I know that *chaos* is a familiar word in English, one that people use all the time. It means confusion, a lot of things happening at once, people bumping into each other, hurry, noise, activity.

But that's not what Chaos meant to the Greeks. The word χάος comes from the same root as the word *chasm*, which means "a big hole in the ground." Far from being a scene of bustling confusion, χάος is nothingness—it's a gap, an abyss. It's related to the Greek word for "yawn."

So if a gap or a hole was all that existed before the world (and everything else) came into being, the question is: a gap between what and what? A hole in what?

Just as the ancient Greeks didn't agree among themselves about what existed before the world, they also didn't agree about what the gap was in. Some of them said that Chaos was surrounded by a circle of flowing water called Okeanos. Others kind of ignored the question.

Still others said that far from being the only thing in existence, Chaos was ruled by a goddess named Eurynome, the daughter of Okeanos and his wife Tethys (but where did *they* come from?). The name Eurynome means "wide-roaming," so she might have been a moon-goddess, since the moon roams across the entire sky. Eurynome wasn't an only child, though. Her mother, Tethys, had more than three thousand children. Among them were the three Graces, goddesses who presided over gracefulness, celebration, singing, dance, merriment, and everything else that brings joy to humanity.

Other Greeks rejected the whole Chaos theory. They said that the first beings were Kronos (Time) and Ananke (Necessity), who must have been something like snakes. They twined themselves around an enormous egg, squeezing it tighter and tighter until it burst, sending the lightest atoms inside it upward to make the sky, and the heavier ones downward to become the earth.

Like Tethys, Ananke was the mother of three daughters, but her girls were gloomier than Tethys's Graces. Ananke's daughters were the three Fates: Lakhesis, who sings about the past; Klotho, who sings about the present; and Atropos, who sings about the future. Klotho spins a thread that represents a human life, Lakhesis measures how long that thread and the life that goes with it will be, and Atropos cuts it where Lakhesis tells her to. Atropos means "unturnable," and once this grim Fate has made up her mind about when someone must die, there's nothing, the Greeks said, that anyone can do about it.

SOME GODS AND GODDESSES YOU MIGHT NOT HAVE HEARD OF AND WHO MIGHT COME IN HANDY:

- Epimetheus, god of excuses
- Kairos, god of luck
- Momos, god of ridicule
- Pasithea, goddess of relaxation
- Peitha, goddess of persuasion (call on her if you're in trouble and Epimetheus doesn't help)
- Pheme, goddess of gossip
- Psamathe, goddess of beaches
- Zelus, god of jealousy

I.
WHERE THINGS COME FROM

DON'T MESS WITH
A SUPERHERO

One story down, sixteen to go. If things keep going this well, I should get through in plenty of time. You don't have any place you have to be, do you?

How about something with a little more action this time? And maybe something funny to help us forget those gloomy Fates?

So however it was that the universe came into being, soon afterward there was an earth, too, with people and animals and plants living on it. There were also gods. Most of them lived on a mountain called Mount Olympos, but they came to earth pretty often, and they appear in a lot of myths, some of which you may know. There were also demi-gods, who were half god and half human. A demi-god named Herakles stars in a lot of myths. You might know him better by his Roman name, Hercules. He was big and strong and heroic.

Or was he? Like most bullies, Herakles couldn't stand to be teased, as he was in this story of two mischievous brothers.

The brothers were named Akmon and Passalos. Their mother was the daughter of the king of Ethiopia and their father was a water spirit. The brothers were small and homely. They were also clever and quick, as well as being thieves and mischief-makers. They climbed trees expertly, which made it easy for them not only to steal fruit but also to escape from the farmers whose crops they ruined.

Their mother despaired that her boys would ever grow up to be good citizens. She constantly told them to behave themselves, but they ignored her. When she tried to punish them, they just laughed. But one warning made them curious.

"Watch out for Burntbottom!" she would say, her voice serious. "Don't bother Burntbottom!"

"Who's Burntbottom?" her sons would ask, but she always refused to say more. She just repeated her warning with a shake of her finger.

So they would shrug and run off to cause more trouble for their neighbors, having a great time and never getting caught.

One summer day, the brothers had wandered farther from home than usual when Akmon noticed someone asleep under a tree. He nudged Passalos and pointed. Curious, they crept close and stared. It was a huge man, and all he wore was a lion-skin. A quiver full of arrows was slung over one of his big shoulders, and he clutched an enormous bow in his fist. He looked like a hunter, taking a nap through the hot part of the day.

A sleeping man was too great a temptation for the brothers to ignore. What could they steal from him? They eyed the lion skin with longing, but its gigantic paws were knotted around the man's neck, and they knew they could never untie them without waking him up. The bow was a beauty, but even if they managed to make away with it, they were much too small to handle such a large weapon.

Then their eyes lit on the arrows. They exchanged a glance and crept closer. Passalos squatted behind the man and slowly, carefully, drew one of the long shafts out of its quiver. He passed it to Akmon and reached for another.

Akmon couldn't help snickering with excitement, and at the sound, the man woke up. Moving more quickly than seemed possible for someone so large, he grabbed the feet of the two brothers, a pair in each hand, and stood up.

Akmon and Passalos were dangling head down, but they weren't worried yet; they had been caught before and had always managed to get away.

"Who are you? How dare you disturb my sleep?" The man's eye fell on the arrow in the grass. "And how *dare* you steal from me?"

"I'm Passalos," Akmon answered.

"I'm Akmon," Passalos said. Even in their dire situation, they couldn't help lying. It was just in their natures.

The huge hunter shook the brothers until their teeth rattled. "And what about my arrows? Do you know what happens to thieves?"

They did. The punishment for stealing something valuable, like arrows, was severe; it could mean the loss of a hand, a severe whipping—even death. But they still weren't worried.

"You can't punish *us*," Passalos said. "Our mother is a princess. And our father is a water spirit."

The man laughed scornfully. "My mother is a princess, too. But my father is no water spirit."

"Not everyone can have a water spirit for a father," Akmon said pityingly. "You just have to learn to live with it."

"Now let us go before you get in trouble," Passalos added.

The man paid no attention. "No, he's not a water spirit." He lifted the brothers higher and boomed right in their faces, "My father is *Zeus!*"

The man whose arrow they had stolen was no mere hunter. He was Herakles, son of the king of the gods, and he was a demi-god, himself. He was stronger than any human alive. He was also known for having quite a temper.

For once, the brothers had no answer. They stared at the demi-god, and then at each other in sudden terror as Herakles bound them by the ankles to each end of a long stick, which he then slung over his shoulder. He turned and strode toward town.

"Where are you taking us?" Passalos managed to squeak.

"To the town well," Herakles said grimly. "I'm going to drown you."

Akmon and Passalos begged and pleaded to be let go. They said that they'd had no intention of keeping the arrows, that they were just having a little fun, but Herakles didn't answer. After a while, they too fell silent as they were carried along, dangling upside down, one in front of their captor, the other behind, both swaying with each step he took.

But they didn't stay silent for long. Since Herakles was so tall and they were so short, their eyes were level with his knees, and being the mischief-makers they were, they couldn't resist sneaking a peek up the lion-skin cloak he wore. Akmon, who was in back, let out a hoot of laughter.

"What is it?" Passalos asked.

At that moment, Herakles switched the pole from one shoulder to the other, and this time, Passalos was hanging behind him. As he bounced along, his head bobbing, he too looked up under the lion skin, and he saw what his brother had already noticed.

Herakles must have been hunting in the nude earlier in the day, and his rear end had gotten sunburned.

"Burntbottom!" Passalos jeered.

"Burntbottom!" Akmon joined in.

Herakles tried to ignore them, but as they laughed and teased, his face turned bright red. He wasn't used to people making fun of him. Finally, he bellowed, "SHUT UP!"

Up on Mount Olympos, Herakles's father, Zeus, heard the angry shout. He looked down to earth. He saw his huge son striding along with two little humans bobbing on the ends of a pole over his shoulder, both of them laughing, and Herakles glowering and looking almost as though he was going to cry. The king of the gods burst out laughing. The other deities ran over to see what was so funny, and soon the sky echoed with their laughter.

Herakles pretended not to hear and kept walking, his face turning redder and redder, until he reached the town square. Keeping his captives' ankles bound together, he slipped them off the pole and dropped them over the side of the well.

Zeus decided to reward Akmon and Passalos for providing the Olympians with so much amusement. He threw a spell down to the earth, and as the brothers fell, their faces flattened. Hair grew all over their bodies, and long tails sprouted from their behinds. Their legs and feet grew so thin that the ropes slipped off their ankles, and they grabbed the stone walls of the well just before they hit the water.

The brothers had always been good climbers, but even they were surprised at how quickly and easily they pulled themselves up and out. But no one was more surprised than Herakles, for instead of two human boys, what scampered out of the well were the first monkeys the world had ever seen.

THERE'S MORE THAN ONE
WAY TO SKIN A LION

The most famous stories about Herakles tell about his "twelve labors," twelve seemingly impossible tasks that he had to accomplish. The first was to kill a lion that was terrorizing the city of Nemea.

This was no ordinary lion. Like a werewolf, the Nemean lion couldn't be harmed by most weapons; his magical fur was invincible to ordinary spears and arrows. He dragged women into his lair in order to lure men into it. When the men approached his cave, they saw what appeared to be an injured woman lying there. When they tried to rescue her, the woman suddenly turned into a lion and devoured them.

Herakles finally killed the Nemean lion, either by clubbing and then strangling him or by shooting an arrow into his open mouth. From then on, the hero always wore the lion's skin as a cloak.

IF IT ISN'T ONE THING, IT'S ANOTHER

Did you like the tale about Herakles and the brothers who turned into monkeys? It always cracks me up to think of those little guys peeking up Herakles's robe.

Sorry, didn't mean to lose it like that. It's not a very realistic story, and I don't think anyone ever thought it really happened. It was just a story to explain why monkeys sometimes act like naughty children. And maybe to show that the big strong guy doesn't always win.

I don't know if the ancient Greeks believed the one I'm about to tell you, either. Most of them probably thought this story was hilarious, but things have changed, and some people might find it upsetting now. You make up your mind which you think it is. Maybe both?

So this myth is about Salmakis. She was a nymph, a kind of humanlike girl that lives in the wild. There were many different kinds of nymphs: The ones called dryads protected trees, oreads protected mountains (I'm thinking about telling a story later about an oread), and naiads lived in and protected streams and rivers and ponds.

Either nymphs don't live where we are right now or else they've gone extinct. I wish there were still some around. It would be nice to have some company. Oh, well, can't be helped. And with any luck, I'll be with Eurydice soon, and then I won't be lonely anymore.

Salmakis was a naiad—a water nymph. The way she acted would have been unthinkable for a well-brought-up girl in ancient Greece, and probably would be today, for all I know. But by behaving badly, she got what she wanted—or did she? You decide.

The land of Anatolia is in what is now Turkey, a country very close to Greece. A lot of Greeks lived there in my day. In Anatolia, there once existed a marvelous pond. Its waters were so clear that a visitor standing at the edge could see its bottom as clearly as if only air lay above it. No spiky grasses or slimy moss grew on the earth and rocks around it, only soft grass as inviting as the finest couch.

Most nymphs liked hunting and other outdoor sports. Salmakis lived in this pond and was its guardian spirit, and she was the only nymph who never picked up a bow and arrow, never joined in a hunt led by the goddess Artemis, never practiced throwing a spear. As they were leaving on a hunt, the other nymphs would call out to her: "Salmakis, it's a beautiful day! Please come with us; you'll have a good time, we promise!"

And she would always answer, "No, thanks. I feel like a swim today" or "It looks like rain; you go on without me." After a while, the nymphs stopped asking, which was just fine with Salmakis. She would watch them come back in the evening, dirty and disheveled, sometimes limping from a wound made by a stray arrow or the tusk of a boar, and wonder what they could possibly find fun about hunting. She preferred to sit at the water's edge and gaze at her own reflection as she combed out her long hair, pondering whether it looked better up or down, whether a center part or one on the side suited her face more, whether she should encourage her hair to curl around her temples or clip it back.

One day, Salmakis decided to pick some flowers to twine in her long locks. She waded out of the water and poked among the bushes to see what was in bloom. She happened to glance up just as a boy emerged from the forest and threw himself down, as if exhausted, at the edge of her pond. She was about to scold him for trespassing when she paused and looked at him. He was *so* handsome. He was almost as handsome as she was pretty, she thought. Luckily, she still held her comb, so she arranged her hair in the most becoming way possible, straightened her dress, and approached him, despite the fact that in her time and place, it would have been shocking for a girl—even a nymph—to talk to a boy her parents didn't know.

When the youth saw her, he sprang to his feet, looking even handsomer when he blushed. Salmakis didn't know it, but the boy's father was the messenger god, Hermes, and his mother was Aphrodite, the goddess of love. The youth was named Hermaphroditos after both his parents. He lived in a nearby mountain range and was on a walking trip, exploring the region.

Hermaphroditos had been raised by naiads, so he was familiar with their ways. He guessed that Salmakis was the guardian spirit of the pond at whose edge he had stopped.

"Please excuse me," he said. "I hope I'm not trespassing."

Salmakis took a step closer. "Oh, no." She smiled at him. "You're welcome to drink and take a rest here."

Something about her made Hermaphroditos uneasy, but he couldn't very well refuse her hospitality without being rude, so he thanked her and squatted by the pond. He cupped his fingers and drank some of the clear water, and then he rose. "Well," he said. "Thank you very much. I'll be on my way now."

But Salmakis was so smitten with Hermaphroditos that she ran up and threw her arms around his neck. "Oh, please, don't go!" she cried. "Why don't you stay with me? We could get married and you could live here forever!"

Hermaphroditos jumped back, freeing himself from her embrace. "Married? Why—why—I don't even know you! What are you talking about? I'm sorry if I said something that made you think—I don't know what you're—I'd better leave."

Salmakis managed to calm herself. "I'm sorry," she said. "You can't leave so soon; everyone would say I hadn't been hospitable, and that would shame me. Please stay a little longer. I'll go away and leave you in peace." He hesitated, since he really was nice and didn't want to be discourteous, and Salmakis took a few steps away. "See? I'm going. Stay as long as you like. Clean the road dust from your clothes. I'll just go for a walk and come back when you've left."

She disappeared into the woods, but she didn't go far. Instead, she knelt behind a shrub and parted its branches so that she could gaze at him.

Hermaphroditos, thinking he was alone and unobserved, took off his sandals. He waded into the pond to relieve the blisters that had arisen during his hike. The cool water felt so good that he walked in up to his knees and then dove under the water. He came up with his dark curls hanging down his neck and his wet lashes looking even longer than they had when dry.

Salmakis couldn't contain herself. He was just too handsome! Forgetting her promise not to return to her pond until Hermaphroditos had left, she ran from her hiding place and jumped into the water. She grabbed the startled boy and hugged him tight. She kissed him again and again as he struggled to get away, twisting and turning, kicking out with his feet and trying to free his arms from her grasp. But he had as much chance of getting away from the nymph as a snake has of escaping an eagle's talons.

Salmakis shouted, "I've won! I've won! He's mine!"

"Let go of me, you crazy girl!" Hermaphroditos sputtered over a mouthful of water that went down the wrong way.

But she clung to him all the tighter and called out, "Gods, please grant that the two of us will never be parted! Keep us together forever!"

The gods granted her wish, although (as often happens) not exactly in the way she meant. Their two bodies joined together as one, and Hermaphroditos, who had entered the pond as two separate people, emerged from it as a new being: half man and half woman.

DON'T BELIEVE EVERYTHING YOU READ

This myth appeared later than most and seems to be a comic story about marriage. In one version of the myth, the encounter between Hermaphroditos and Salmakis occurred on the fourth day of the month, which was considered a lucky day to get married. Hermes and Aphrodite, the parents of Hermaphroditos, were sometimes worshipped as a couple, and both were called upon to bless brides on their wedding day. This story might have been told to amuse wedding guests, but people today might not find it so funny to read about someone being kissed and hugged without their permission.

THE TRUTH WILL OUT

So you liked that one? Not too silly? Not upsetting? Okay if I keep going? This will be my fourth tale, and I don't want to waste any time.

You know, not many people come through the woods here, and I was just about to give up hope when I saw you. Some of the people who pass by don't even hear me when I try to get them to stop. A couple times they've built fires on top of me, when the ground is wet and they want a dry surface. Do they ever think that it might hurt to have a fire on top of your head? No. I'm just a rock to them.

So let's get on with it. Here's a tale that's a little more serious. It's all about truth-telling, which was as important in my time as it is for you modern folks.

A lot of things have changed in the past few thousand years, though. In my day, we didn't have all the things you people can't seem to live without. We had some kinds of metal, but it was really expensive. Only rich people could afford anything made of glass. Most cooking pots, serving ware, dishes, cups, lamps, religious objects, statues, and other things we used in our everyday lives were made from clay.

So it's no wonder the first potter was an important character in the tales that my people told. This potter's name was Prometheus, and he was a Titan. Titans are hard to explain. They're immortal, so they're a kind of god, but they came in between the really early gods—like Tethys and Ananke—and the Olympians that most people think of when they talk about Greek gods.

One thing that hasn't changed since my time is that everyone likes it when a practical joke is played on someone really important. I think that people who listened to this next tale probably enjoyed seeing the great Prometheus being fooled, even if he eventually figured out that someone was trying to trick him.

Prometheus is best known for being the guy who created the human race. He made his people out of clay and stole fire from the heavens as a gift to them. He's still being punished in the underworld for that. Another story tells how he once fooled Zeus into accepting a sacrifice that wasn't very good and kept the better one for himself. So it's odd that despite stealing from the gods and cheating their king, Prometheus valued honesty so highly that he decided to make a *daimona* (a female *daimon*, or spirit) out of clay, to be a kind of living symbol of Truth.

Even today, it's hard to make a full-size clay statue. The potter has to form the parts of the body separately and join them together after they're baked, or fired, as potters call it. Large pieces sometimes shatter in the high heat of the kiln—the very, very hot oven they're hardened in—and the different parts shrink as the water is baked out of them. The potter has to calculate the shrinkage precisely, so that pieces that fit together before firing will still fit together afterward. Prometheus was really good at this, obviously, and he also had a skilled helper, named Dolos. Even so, it took a long time before he was ready to put the finishing touches on his beautiful statue of Truth.

Just as Prometheus was about to settle down to work on it again, he received a summons from Zeus. It was impossible to ignore a command from the king of the gods, but

Prometheus hated to leave his work when it was so close to completion.

"Don't worry," said Dolos. "You've already done the hard part. I'll finish it up while you're gone."

Prometheus wasn't sure he should allow that. The apprentice came of good parents; his father was the air and his mother was Gaia, the earth. But the rest of Dolos's family didn't exactly inspire confidence: His brothers and sisters included Pain, Anger, Lamentation, and Fear. The potter had another reason to worry. His apprentice's name means "trickery."

As the Titan hesitated, Dolos said, "I'll do a good job; I promise." So, against his better judgment, Prometheus agreed.

But he had been right to be suspicious, because Dolos had no intention of completing Prometheus's work. He had hatched a plan to make his master look foolish. Why? I don't know. I guess if your name is Trickery, you just like playing tricks. Anyway, as soon as Dolos was sure that the Titan was gone, he set about sculpting a second statue that would be identical to the first one.

Dolos had learned a lot in his apprenticeship with Prometheus, and he was skilled. Tricksters have to be good at what they do, or they don't fool anyone. Under his skilled fingers, the new statue took shape. Like the real statue, this figure was nude, because the ancient Greek word for truth, *aletheia* (αλήθεια), literally means "without concealment." Her face and body were flawless, because the truth is unblemished. She looked beautiful and strong, and she wore an expression of fearlessness.

Dolos worked hard, hoping that Prometheus wouldn't return until he was done. He fit the various pieces—arms, legs, head, torso—to one another so he could see what they'd look like when they were fired and joined together. He was almost through when something happened that ruined his whole plan: He ran out of clay.

What would he do now? Dolos had finished everything but the statue's feet, but he didn't have time to get more clay, because just then, he heard Prometheus approaching. Dolos quickly hid the statue Prometheus had been working on behind a screen and put his own creation in its place. Then he got busy cleaning implements, stacking firewood for the kiln, and sweeping the floor.

When Prometheus entered and surveyed his studio, at first the great potter saw nothing amiss. Suddenly, he realized that, while at first glance his statue looked the same as when he had left it, it seemed to have lost its feet.

"What happened here?" Prometheus asked, too bewildered at first to suspect his helper of doing anything to his work. He leaned in and examined the statue as Dolos held his breath.

When Prometheus straightened, Dolos saw that he was furious. "Did anyone come in while I was gone?" the potter growled. Dolos shook his head. "Did you leave at any time?"

Dolos was too terrified to answer. If Prometheus found out what he had done, he would punish him in ways too terrible to contemplate. Why he hadn't thought about what would happen when his trick was revealed, I don't know. Maybe he'd just been carried away with the thought of how much fun it would be to fool the guy who had created the human race.

Prometheus inspected the statue again, and when he faced his apprentice this time, Dolos could tell that he had figured out what happened. "I can see I taught you well," the Titan said, and Dolos was so relieved at his master's calmness that he let out the breath he had been holding.

"The one you made is behind that screen," he said quickly. "I'll just destroy mine and—"

Now it was Prometheus's turn to shake his head. "No, let's keep it. I'll fire them both in the kiln and breathe life into them, the way I did to make my humans come alive.

25

The statue I made will be called Truth, and yours will be Falsehood. For Falsehood sometimes manages to start a lie circulating, but without feet, she can't move very far, whereas Truth will always spread throughout the land."

WATCH OUT FOR THESE GUYS

A prayer to Athena lists five unpleasant "potters' spirits" who interfere with a potter's work: Syntribos the Crusher, Smaragos the Smasher, Asbetos the Burner, Sabaktes the Shatterer, and Omodamos the Underbaker.

II.
LIFE'S BIG MOMENTS:
BIRTH, LOVE, DEATH

THE BEST GOD

Four down, thirteen to go—I'm almost a quarter of the way there! I can't tell you how good it will feel to apologize to Eurydice for being such an idiot. Have you ever done anything stupid? I mean really, really stupid? Sometimes you can fix it, but sometimes there's nothing you can do, right? You can't undo it. All you can do is apologize and hope the other person is nicer than you were stupid. That's how it was in my day, and I bet that's how it is today.

I know that parts of your lives are different from mine in ways I can't even imagine, but from what I've seen and overheard through the centuries, some of the most important things about humans haven't changed much at all. You still wonder about life, death, why people fall in love, how we stay alive in a tough world—that kind of thing. Stories can be a good way to answer those questions. A lot of times, the Greeks answered a question about how humans learned to do something—build a fire, say, or make pots—by claiming that the gods taught them. But why would the gods give these gifts to humanity?

Sometimes love was the reason. In the myths told by my people, the gods and goddesses often fell in love with humans. Usually it was the beauty of the man or woman that attracted them. The sun god, Apollo, was a little different from the others. Once, he fell in love with a girl whose looks weren't the prime attraction, and out of their love came great gifts to humanity.

Apollo happened to be traveling in central Greece when an unusual sight caught his eye. A young woman had trapped a lion in a net and was wrestling with it. Her blond hair whipped around her head as she dodged the animal's huge teeth and slashing claws. Normally, Apollo would have simply grabbed her and tried to kiss her; but something about the girl—her strength, her skill, the fact that she liked to wrestle lions, who knows?—intrigued him. He left her to finish her battle and sought out the famous half-horse, half-human centaur, Chiron, who lived in a cave nearby.

"There's only one maiden in this area who fits that description," Chiron said after Apollo told him what he had seen. "It must be Kyrene, one of the daughters of the king around these parts. There's been talk of a lion attacking cattle, and I wouldn't be surprised if Kyrene took it on herself to deal with it. She had the beast trapped in a net and was wrestling it, you say?"

Apollo nodded, and Chiron laughed. "Sounds like Kyrene. She's so strong and so skilled at the hunt, she probably boasted that she didn't even need a spear and could kill the lion with her bare hands. But...." He paused. "Do I have your permission to speak freely?"

"You do," Apollo said.

"Kyrene has little interest in marrying." That was understandable. While it was rare for a princess to enjoy any kind of sport, it was acceptable so long as she didn't neglect her responsibilities at home. But ancient Greek girls in general—and princesses in particular—had a duty to marry, and marriage would have brought an end to Kyrene's hunting. It would have been unheard of for a woman to leave her husband and children to spend all day at the risky business of tracking and killing ferocious beasts. So Kyrene had to choose one or the other—married life or hunting—and she had chosen hunting.

Apollo must have shown his disappointment, for the centaur, who was a seer—that is, someone who can predict the future—said, "Don't despair. I see that the two of you will be married not long from now. You will live together in a far-off land, where you and Kyrene will have two sons. One will become a famous seer, and the other will bring wonderful gifts to humanity."

This was encouraging. Apollo hurried from Chiron's cave back to the plain where the girl had been wrestling the lion. The beast lay tied up behind the maiden, who was receiving the congratulations and thanks of the farmers whose sheep and cattle would now be safe.

Apollo introduced himself to the princess and told her that, unlike mortal men, he was fine with having a wife who hunted. Kyrene was so dazzled at the sight of the god, and at the prospect of continuing to do what she loved to do *and* having a family, that she agreed to marry him that very day.

Off they went to the African country of Libya, where everything happened as the wise centaur had foreseen. Kyrene became Libya's queen, well loved by her people and by her immortal husband. Their first son did grow up to become a seer. He foresaw his own death if he joined an adventurous group of sailors called the Argonauts, but he joined them anyway. I was an Argonaut and I knew him, and sure enough, he was killed by a boar during a voyage. Too bad. He was a nice guy.

But it was their second son who made a name for himself. What that name was isn't clear. He's called Anthokos (Flowering), Nomios (God of Shepherds), and Argaios (the Argive, a person from the region of Argos), but he's usually known as Aristaios—The Best.

What did Aristaios do to earn this title? Was he a brave warrior, vanquishing his enemies in ferocious battles? Did he bring renown to his country by composing wonderful music, writing beautiful poetry, sculpting lovely statues? Did he honor the gods, causing them to shower Libya with favors?

No. What made this prince the best person ever was that he invented bee-keeping, cheese-making, and how to make olive oil.

These gifts might not seem terribly important to you. Honey is delicious, but if you don't have any, you can always use sugar, right? Wrong, at least in ancient Greece. Sugar didn't reach Greece until the fourth century BCE at the earliest, and it remained scarce and expensive until modern times. Honey was really our only sweetener. It was also used in medicine, because it kills some germs, and in religious festivals.

And cheese—again, it's fine, but what's the big deal? The big deal is that a lot of people in my time didn't have much to eat, and cheese concentrates just about all the nutrition of milk into an easily stored form.

Olive oil is good for you, too, but in my day, people also used it to make soap, perfume, medicine, and other important things. Rich people could have light in their homes after sundown, thanks to lamps filled with olive oil. You still hold the Olympic Games, where the winners are given medals, right? In my day, the winners were crowned with olive wreaths, and at other games, they were often awarded huge jars of olive oil. That shows you how precious it was.

So Aristaios deserves all the admiration we used to give him. I'm sorry nobody seems to know of him today.

GEOGRAPHY

To the ancient Greeks, "Libya" meant North Africa, not today's country of that name. The Greeks also referred to much of central and southern Africa as Ethiopia.

BUT DOES SHE REALLY LOVE YOU?

So that makes five, right? I'm starting to get anxious. See how low the sun is getting? It's shining in my eyes. Do you mind moving over to make a shadow?

How about a change of pace? You okay with something sad? My people specialized in sad stories. This myth starts with yet another love story between a human and a god. We were kind of obsessed with that idea, I don't know why. When a god falls in love with a mortal, there's no guarantee of a happy ending.

Usually, the human was fine with leaving his or her life—including a family, if any—and going off with the god. If you think about it, it would be hard to say no, wouldn't it? Kyrene was happy to marry Apollo, but this tale is different. This time, the human didn't just trot off when the immortal beckoned; the man who caught a goddess's eye in this myth took some persuading. It would have been better for him if—oh, never mind. Listen and see what you think.

Prokris was the daughter of the king of Athens. She was happily married to a man named Kephalos, who often went hunting early in the morning. One day, as Eos, the Titan goddess of the dawn, was bringing light to the world, she saw Kephalos as he headed into the woods and immediately fell in love with him. She flew down and dazzled him with her goddessly splendor.

"Come away with me," Eos begged. "I'll ask Zeus to make you immortal, and we'll be together forever."

Kephalos was tempted by the goddess's beauty, and especially by the thought of living forever, but he loved Prokris very much. So he told Eos that he wouldn't go with her. He just couldn't be untrue to his wife.

Eos was furious when Kephalos refused her for love of a mere mortal. "You're a fool," she told him. "Your wife doesn't care for you. Why, she would be unfaithful to you for nothing—a trinket."

"I don't believe you," Kephalos said, but the goddess seemed so sure of herself that a small flame of doubt flickered within him. *Did* Prokris really love him as much as he loved her?

Eos saw his uneasiness. "I can prove it," she told him. "I'll change your appearance, and you can go to your wife pretending to be a stranger. Offer her a gift if she'll be unfaithful to her husband, and see what she does."

Kephalos was reluctant, but once Eos had lit the fire of doubt in his mind, he had to do as she suggested or forever be tormented wondering if his wife really loved him. So he allowed the goddess to disguise him. Once Eos was satisfied no one would recognize him, she gave Kephalos a golden crown and told him to offer it to his wife if she would go off with him.

Kephalos returned home and entered his house, where Prokris sat weaving. He expected her to be frightened, since he looked nothing like himself, and at first, she *was* frightened. She started to run away, but he called out and begged her to stay. When she saw how handsome the stranger was, and especially when he got down on one knee and held the golden crown out to her, she waited to hear what he had to say.

Kephalos cleared his throat. "Lovely lady," he said, hoping his wife wouldn't recognize his voice, "you don't know me, but I have loved you from afar for a long time. I beg you to leave your husband and come away with me. I'll treat you like a queen. Here, take this crown and wear it to show that you'll accept me."

Did Prokris hesitate? Did she think of her husband, to whom she had sworn to be faithful?

Apparently not. She took the crown from the hand of the "stranger" and placed it on her dark curls.

Kephalos couldn't believe his eyes. He stood up, enraged. Eos, who was watching from a hiding place, changed him back to his normal appearance. When Prokris recognized her husband, she laughed nervously, trying to hide her embarrassment and guilt. "I knew all along it was you," she said. "Here, take this silly crown back. I don't want it. I was just going along with your joke."

But Kephalos didn't believe her. Without a word, he strode from his house, heartbroken and furious. He went off with Eos and eventually they had a son. But he was never really happy. He missed Prokris and his old life.

Prokris was so ashamed of her willingness to be false to her husband that she couldn't bear to stay where people would mock her. She ran away to the island of Crete, where she met the famous King Minos. He lived in a palace where a great maze hid a monstrous half-man, half-bull called the Minotaur. The king fell in love with Prokris and gave her wondrous gifts: a spear that never missed its mark and a hound named Lailaps that never failed to catch his quarry. The goddess Artemis herself, mistress of the hunt, had given the spear and the dog to Minos. (Remember Lailaps and the spear; they're in another story I want to tell you.)

After a while, Prokris grew worried that Minos's wife, who was a powerful priestess as well as being the queen, would become jealous and kill her. So she disguised herself as a boy and, calling herself Pterelas, escaped back to Athens, taking the hound and the spear with her.

Meanwhile, Kephalos had never forgotten Prokris. After a few years, he left Eos (who had apparently forgotten her promise to make him immortal) and spent all his time hunting, roaming aimlessly from place to place. He missed his wife more and more every day and regretted that he had ever tempted her with the golden crown. In his wanderings, he met up with a boy named Pterelas and they became hunting companions. Kephalos never suspected that the handsome boy was really his beloved wife, and she was too ashamed to reveal her true identity to him.

One day, Kephalos said to the boy, "It's no wonder you're such a successful hunter. Your spear and dog are unbeatable. What would you take for them?"

Prokris said they weren't for sale, which only made Kephalos more eager to buy them. Finally, she said, "There's only one thing I'd trade them for."

"What's that?" Kephalos asked.

"Love," she said, and bursting into tears, she told him that she was his wife.

Kephalos was overjoyed to have Prokris back. Each forgave the other, and together they spent many days hunting with the enchanted spear and hound. (Doesn't that sound wonderful? Oh, I hope that Eurydice forgives me as easily!) But after a while, Artemis noticed Kephalos and Prokris going after game in the woods, and it irritated her to know that mortals were passing around her precious gifts. Minos had given Lailaps and the spear to Prokris, and then Prokris had offered them to Kephalos—all for something as unimportant as human love.

One night, the goddess decided to punish the two for failing to respect her and her gifts, and she entered Prokris's dreams.

"Where do you think your husband goes every morning when he leaves the house before daylight?" she asked the sleeping Prokris. "Do you really think he's hunting? Nobody loves hunting that much! No, he's still in love with

Eos, and he meets her when she arrives on the earth to bring the dawn. That's why he gets up so early."

"I don't believe you," Prokris said, but she felt uneasy, just as Kephalos had when Eos had told him his wife would be unfaithful. *Was* her husband really hunting each morning? Why did he leave the house in time to greet the dawn? Why not wait until daylight?

The goddess laughed. "See for yourself," she said.

When Prokris awoke, her heart was pounding. As she lay still, worrying about what the goddess had said and wondering if it was true, she felt Kephalos rise. She couldn't stand not knowing where he was going, so once he was out the door, she got up, too. She put on a dark cloak so she'd be hard to see in the dim early-morning light, and followed him.

Kephalos had no idea that Prokris was even awake, much less trailing him through the woods. He moved quietly in the semi-darkness, the magic spear in his hand, the magic hound by his side. He hoped to spot one of the animals that are active at dawn—a deer, perhaps.

Suddenly, something brushed against a branch. Lailaps whipped his head around and growled, and Kephalos, thinking the hound had spotted prey, flung his spear into the woods. He heard a moan and ran to where his target had fallen. He gasped in horror at the sight of his beloved wife, who lay on the ground with his spear in her chest. He cradled her in his arms, calling her name, but there was nothing he could do. She gave him one last, loving look, took one last breath, and died.

Kephalos was so distraught that he didn't even care when he was ordered to leave his homeland and never return for the crime of murdering his wife. He wandered through many countries, eventually settling on an island that was renamed Kephalonia in his honor. Memories of Prokris haunted him, as did her ghost, who came to him in the semi-darkness of dawn and looked at him reproachfully.

Finally, Kephalos could no longer stand the terrible guilt he felt—for testing Prokris with the golden crown, for going off with Eos, and especially for throwing his spear without seeing what he was aiming at, thereby killing his beloved hunting companion and wife. He climbed up onto a cliff and flung himself into the sea. With his last breath, he called out, "Pterelas!" for that was the name Prokris had been using when he found her again.

CAN WE JUST BE FRIENDS?

Romances between Greek gods and humans rarely had happy endings, partly because of that irritating habit humans have of dying, while gods live forever. The dawn goddess, Eos, thought she had figured a way out of that particular problem when she asked Zeus to grant eternal life to her boyfriend (not Kephalos; a different one). Unfortunately, Eos forgot to ask for eternal youth for him as well. The result was that while she stayed young and active, he grew older and older and more and more bent, and his voice got creakier and creakier, until he shriveled up and turned into a cicada.

APPLES AND LOVE

Oh, dear. That myth is even sadder than I'd remembered. And it reminds me of my own problems. I didn't trust the gods of the underworld, and look what happened to me. Kephalos didn't trust Prokris, and Prokris didn't trust Kephalos, and they both wound up dead. Kephalos couldn't live with his mistake, and he jumped off a cliff. I couldn't forgive myself, so I lost my mind and wandered into mortal danger—a kind of death by nymph.

For story seven, let's have something a bit more cheery. All right?

Apples play a big role in the love stories of my people, the ancient Greeks. I have no idea why. Maybe it's because they're sweet. Oh, I know, other fruits are sweet, but we didn't have many back then. Some people had a picnic here once, about a hundred years ago, I think, and they were eating this big green thing that was red inside, with black seeds—you know what I'm talking about? A watermelon? I guess you're right. Whatever it was, a lot of the juice dripped on me, and it was amazing. The ants and bees that got stuck on my face weren't so amazing, but it was worth it.

Where was I? Oh, right. The apple tree is special to Aphrodite, the goddess of love. Maybe that's why people think of apples when they tell stories about love. Prince

Paris gave an apple to Aphrodite in order to win Helen, the most beautiful woman in the world, and that's what started the Trojan War. In another myth, a young man threw golden apples in front of a fleet-footed princess named Atalanta during a footrace, so that she would lose the race and have to marry him.

The apple that you're going to hear about, which a young man named Akontios used to trick a beautiful girl named Kydippe, was just an ordinary apple. It wasn't made of gold and it wasn't the prize in a goddess beauty contest, but it had its own kind of magic.

Akontios was a handsome young farmer from the small island of Keos, near the even smaller island of Delos. Delos was the birthplace of Artemis, goddess of the moon and of the hunt, and her twin brother, the sun god Apollo, so it was a sacred place. Every four years, people from all over the ancient Greek world came to the festival of Artemis to worship her and marvel at her temple.

Young men and women were usually kept apart, and such festivals were a popular way to meet. Artemis, who had sworn never to marry, was the guardian of unmarried women. Many marriages were arranged at her temple, where girls would feel they were under the protection of a goddess who would look out for them.

One year, Akontios decided to go to the festival. Maybe he would meet a nice girl to marry, and even if he didn't, he'd be sure to have a good time. So he borrowed a boat from a fisherman and rowed the short distance to Delos.

When Akontios climbed out of the boat, he was astonished at what he saw. People from all over Greece and beyond were filling tiny Delos, which is only a bit larger than a square mile in your modern measurements. Countless wares were for sale, from food and drink to trinkets and clothing. From the stadium came the roar of people watching footraces, wrestling matches, and other games held in honor of the goddess. And still more boats arrived and unloaded more and more people onto the island, until it seemed like it was going to sink.

A simple country boy, Akontios was overwhelmed, wandering and staring at all the wonders, clutching his small wallet of coins. He bought three apples from a vendor, though their price made him gasp. He ate two, and tucked the third into the folds of his tunic for later.

He found a crowd of people exclaiming at the sight of the huge, intricate altar in front of the temple of Artemis. Some of the worshippers were making sacrifices and asking the goddess for a favor. Others were swearing solemn oaths—some to marry a certain person, others to call an end to a feud, still others to live a more honorable life. The Greeks took very seriously any promise made at a temple, especially one as holy as that of Artemis at Delos.

"Really something, isn't it?" asked a friendly voice behind him. Akontios turned and saw a prosperous-looking young man of about his own age.

"I've never seen anything like it," Akontios said.

"There isn't anything like it in the whole world." The young man spoke with an Athenian accent. "Apollo, god of the arts, made the altar himself from the antlers and horns of animals killed by his sister Artemis."

Akontios approached the altar and put out a reverent hand to touch one of the antlers. As he did so, he saw a beautiful girl standing on the steps of the temple, making a sacrifice. The girl was even more spectacular than the altar. Her large eyes shone with intelligence, and her hair, tied back in a simple knot, was thick and wavy. Her face was as lovely as that of the statue of the goddess herself.

The Athenian noticed where Akontios was looking and laughed. "No point in losing your heart over that one, my friend. That's Kydippe. Her father is a nobleman of Athens, and he won't give her in marriage to any suitor who isn't well born and rich. I'm afraid a man with no money from—where did you say? Keos?—wouldn't be good enough." The Athenian's eye swept over Akontios's simple tunic, his plain sandals, his work-roughened hands.

Akontios hardly heard him as he stared at the lovely girl. How to meet her? It would be highly improper for him to approach her. High-born Greek women were kept so strictly secluded, many of them left home only to attend festivals like this one.

On an impulse, Akontios pulled his last apple out of his tunic. With the knife he always carried, he carved some words into its skin and tossed it at the girl's feet.

Kydippe's maid picked it up, glancing around to see where it had come from. Akontios kept himself hidden behind the intertwined horns of the altar, and after a while, the woman gave up looking and handed the apple to her mistress. Kydippe was about to take a bite out of it when she saw the words that Akontios had carved.

Idly, she read aloud: "I swear by the temple of Artemis that I will marry Akontios." She glanced at her maid. "Who's this Akontios?" The woman shrugged, and Kydippe ate the apple without trying any harder to find out who he was. Akontios's heart sank.

"Nice try," the Athenian said sympathetically.

"Move on, boy," a rough voice said, and Akontios, after one more glance over his shoulder at the beautiful girl, allowed the next group to come and marvel at the temple and its altar. He didn't manage to see Kydippe again, and when the festival was over, he returned to Keos and tried to forget her.

Kydippe went home, too, and her father soon found an eligible young man for her to marry. Most marriages in those days were arranged by the parents of the bride and groom. Hardly anyone expected to be in love with the person they married, so it didn't strike Kydippe as unfair that she had no say in the matter. She prepared for the wedding, but the day before the ceremony was to take place, she fell ill. Not wanting a sickly wife, the prospective groom married someone else. This happened not once but twice more, until three weddings had been called off.

Kydippe's father was worried. His daughter *had* to get married; there were no other options in those days. Girls couldn't get jobs, and a girl of Kydippe's background wouldn't know how to farm or fish or do anything else to earn a living. If she never married, she'd have no one to support her once her parents died.

It was strange, though. When a wedding wasn't being planned, Kydippe was as healthy as any other girl. Could she be pretending to be sick? Her father told his wife to question their daughter closely, but Kydippe denied that she was faking.

"Then what could it be, my darling?" her mother asked. "Are you afraid of getting married?"

"Oh, no," Kydippe said. "I'd have been happy with any of those men that Father chose."

"When you went to the festival on Delos, you didn't make any silly promises to the goddess, did you? You know, Artemis vowed never to marry, and sometimes girls at her festivals get carried away and make the same oath." She noticed her daughter staring at her in shock, and she turned pale. "You did, didn't you?" she exclaimed. "Oh, Kydippe, how could you?"

"No, Mother, no, I didn't swear never to marry. But—" And she recounted the story of the apple carved with the oath to marry someone named Akontios.

Her mother realized that Kydippe had made a solemn promise at the altar, even if she hadn't intended to, and she told her husband what their daughter had done. He was furious, but he knew he didn't have any choice. He had to allow Kydippe to marry this unknown man. He asked far and wide if anyone knew how to find him.

One of his friends had a son who had gone to the festival and remembered meeting a man named Akontios, from an island called Keos. They had chatted by the altar, the young man recalled, and he'd seen Akontios toss an apple to Kydippe. Maybe this was the man she had sworn to marry.

It didn't sound likely, but Kydippe's father was desperate. He sent messengers to Keos, where they found that the only young man named Akontios who fit the description was a simple farmer. He seemed pleasant enough, but the thought of marrying his beloved daughter to someone he didn't know and who wasn't of the social class she'd been born into, was distasteful to her father. He tried once more to marry her to a young man of Athens, one who came with a noble pedigree and a good treasury.

But the day before the wedding, Kydippe fell ill again. She fainted in her mother's arms and remained unconscious as physicians bustled in and out of the house, applying every remedy they could think of. Nothing did any good.

WONDROUS ARTEMIS

Today Artemis is somewhat eclipsed by her flashy brother, the sun god Apollo, but in the ancient world, she was hugely important. Her temple in Ephesus, Turkey, is the largest Greek temple ever built. It made it onto everybody's list of wonders of the ancient world. The poet who put together the most famous of these lists said, "I've seen the wall of the high city of Babylon, which is so wide there's a chariot-track on top of it; and the statue of Zeus near the Alpheus River; and the Hanging Gardens of Babylon; and the great Colossus of the Sun in Alexandria; and the huge pyramids; and the great Mausoleum; but when I saw the temple of Artemis, which reaches to the clouds, those other wonders dimmed in my sight, and I said, 'Except for Mount Olympos itself, the sun has never seen anything as grand as this.'"

Kydippe's father gave up. He told his daughter's most recent fiancé that the wedding was off and sent for Akontios. Akontios couldn't believe his good fortune. He put on his best tunic, borrowed new sandals from a neighbor, and set sail for Athens. He and Kydippe were married the next day, and Akontios made sure that apples were served at the wedding feast.

ALL'S FAIR IN LOVE AND WAR

So Akontios was a little sneaky, but some people in the myths did really bad things to get the one they loved—sometimes even murder. There's a myth about a king's daughter that I don't think gets told much today.

Stop me if you've heard this.

In my day, the most important job qualification for being king was to be the best soldier around. I've learned from what I've overheard lately—oh, say, in the last five hundred years or so—that it's different now. I hear that the rulers of most countries have more to do with things like laws and taxes than with combat, and that even when there's a war, they hardly ever fight. Is this true? It's hard to wrap my mind around.

Anyway, kings who rule by military might usually want to make sure that their daughters marry men who are good fighters. Perhaps that's why so many myths and fairy tales are about a young man who has to perform a valiant deed in order to gain a princess's hand in marriage. Winning a challenge would show both strength and courage, proving that the man was worthy of his bride and could protect her and their children.

In these stories, the woman doesn't usually get involved in the challenge, but in this one, a girl changed the outcome of the contest.

King Sithon of Thrace had two daughters, Pallene and Rhoeteia. He was determined that his girls should marry men who were strong and brave, so when Pallene, the older girl, reached marriageable age, Sithon declared that he would give her only to a man who could beat him in a swordfight. That way, he would be assured that his daughter's husband was strong enough to protect her, their family, and their kingdom.

Potential grooms came to Thrace from all over the Greek world. Some of these men were eager to marry this intelligent, beautiful girl from a powerful family, while others were more interested in showing off what great swordsmen they were. One after another, all of them died at the king's hands.

Pallene grew more and more eager to leave home and start her own life. She couldn't inherit the kingdom; women weren't allowed to rule countries in those days. She was frightened of her stern father, and she hardly knew her mother, who was a nymph and spent most of her time in the woods. Her closest companions were her sister and the palace guard who had taken care of the princesses since they were small. He loved them as if they were his own daughters, and they loved and trusted him.

King Sithon eventually became too old for combat, and suitors stopped coming to the palace. No warrior wanted to win a fight only to hear people say that if Sithon had been younger, the contender would certainly have lost. So despite the attraction of the princesses and the large kingdom, potential husbands stayed away.

But one day, two suitors, Dryas and Kleitos, unexpectedly appeared at the palace and presented themselves to fight for Pallene's hand. King Sithon felt he was nearing the end of his days, and besides, he could use a young man in the family to help control his kingdom. So he was finally ready to allow someone to become his son-in-law.

"Never fear," he told the two men. "You won't have to feel the shame of fighting an old man. I have a new plan, one that will give honor to the victor. I will unveil it at dinner tonight."

Pallene and her sister, who had given up on ever marrying, were thrilled at the news of the arrival of these suitors. Rhoeteia helped Pallene dress for dinner with particular care—twining fresh flowers in her dark hair, using the burnt end of a twig to line her eyes with charcoal—as they tried to guess their father's plan.

That night, they entered the banquet hall under the watchful eyes of their parents and their beloved guard. Quietly, they took their places at the women's table. As musicians played pipes and stringed instruments, a juggler and an acrobat performed, and dogs yipped and fought over scraps, the girls discussed the strangers.

"They're both handsome," Rhoeteia said.

Pallene agreed, but her eye had been caught by Kleitos. He *was* good-looking, but more than that, he listened courteously when others spoke, and when the performers circulated among the diners with their bowls, he generously gave them large helpings off his plate.

"I like that one," Pallene said. "The shorter one, with the light hair."

Eros, the god of love, happened to be there with a quiver full of the golden arrows he used to make people fall in love. Being in a good mood, he decided to help the princess, so he shot two of his golden arrows: one into Pallene's heart and the other into the heart of Kleitos, just as he glanced at Pallene. Both fell instantly in love.

When King Sithon stood, the room fell silent. "Honored guests," he began, "here we have two suitors for the hand of my daughter Pallene. I am an old man—" He waited modestly until the cries of "No, no!" and "You're still in your prime!" died down. "It's time for the girl to be married, but her husband must be worthy of her." He turned to Dryas and Kleitos. "In three days, the two of you will fight one another from chariots. Whoever wins will become my son-in-law. Whoever loses," he looked around the room, "will die." The king sat down as low murmurs and buzzing conversation rose around him.

Pallene had lost her appetite. A strong, tall man would stand the best chance of winning such a swordfight, and Kleitos was smaller than Dryas. She knew that she could not change her father's mind once he had made a decision. All she could do was pray that somehow Kleitos would be victorious. And over the next few days, the more Pallene saw of the two, the more she liked Kleitos—and the less she liked Dryas.

The night before the chariot race, Pallene didn't sleep at all. How could she bear it if Dryas won the fight? Toward morning, she wandered into the garden. The stars moved overhead, and when dawn broke in the east, she sat on a stone bench and sobbed quietly.

"What's wrong, princess?" The familiar voice of her old guard broke in on Pallene's thoughts. At first, she was reluctant to confide in him, but he managed to coax the truth from her. "You're sure you wish to marry this man?" he asked.

"Oh, yes." She started to cry again.

The guard stood up. "I'll see to it." His voice was firm. "Don't worry. If this is the man you want to marry, you will marry him. Just leave it to me." He hesitated. "It will take a little money."

"Whatever you need." Pallene handed him the pouch of coins she wore around her waist. She didn't care what his plan was, as long as Kleitos won. "If it's not enough, just tell me."

The guard hurried away, and Pallene went to the field of combat. People had been gathering since the night before to get a good view of the contest, and now they were shouting and cheering. The princess climbed up to the royal seats, where her mother and sister awaited her. She was eager to learn what the guard's plan was, but frightened at the same time. What if it didn't work? How could she bear to see Kleitos killed?

When King Sithon strode onto the sandy field, leading a white bull, the crowd fell silent. The king recited a prayer to the gods, dedicating this fight to them and begging them to let the more worthy man win. Then he drew his gleaming knife across the bull's throat, spilling its blood over the high stone altar and onto the sand as an offering to the gods.

Pallene looked around anxiously but didn't see the guard anywhere. Had he failed her? She shuddered. "What is it, sister?" Rhoeteia asked. Pallene shook her head. She wished no harm to Dryas, but she couldn't stand the thought that Kleitos's blood would probably be spilled on that sand in a few short minutes.

Sithon joined his wife and daughters in the stands, and the spectators rose to their feet, cheering wildly, as two chariots appeared at opposite ends of the field. The opponents climbed in behind their drivers, each clutching his sword in one hand and his shield in the other. Then the crowd fell silent. Their bronze helmets covered most of the fighters' faces, but everyone could sense their grim determination.

When Sithon shouted, "Go!" the drivers slapped their reins on the horses' backs, and the animals took off. The spectators shouted themselves hoarse with excitement as the horses picked up speed, tearing across the field.

All of a sudden, one of the huge wheels on Dryas's chariot began wobbling dangerously. But Dryas's driver, instead of trying to slow the horses, dropped the reins and held onto the edge of the vehicle with both hands, as though aware that something terrible was about to happen. Then he jumped out, leaving Dryas alone in the chariot. Dryas flung his sword and shield away and grabbed desperately at the reins to try to stop the horses.

Pallene leaped to her feet in horror, her hand at her throat. Kleitos shouted at his own driver to stop, but before the man could react, Dryas's chariot crashed onto its side, flinging its passenger onto the ground. Kleitos instantly jumped down and stabbed his rival, killing him.

It all happened so fast that Pallene was bewildered. Kleitos had won and that thrilled her, but why hadn't Dryas's driver checked his chariot to make sure it was sound before they climbed into it? Why had he jumped out instead of reining in the horses as soon as the wheel started to wobble?

The crowd ran to congratulate Kleitos and to carry Dryas's corpse off the field. Preparing to burn his body in a magnificent ceremony, they built a huge funeral pyre. A man who had fallen in such a contest should be honored.

Pallene tried to rejoice at Kleitos's victory, but she couldn't. Her feeling of dread grew when she saw two men walk over to the broken chariot and crouch down next to the wheel. They pointed at something and spoke in excited tones.

Then one of the men ran to where Pallene stood with her family and knelt before her father. "Sir," he said, "someone has tampered with that chariot."

"Tampered?" Sithon asked sharply. "What do you mean?"

"The pins that were supposed to hold the wheel to the axle—they're not there. Someone took them out. The wheel jolted loose as soon as the chariot hit a stone."

"Bring Kleitos and both drivers to me," the king ordered.

Soon the three men stood before Sithon, Dryas's charioteer looking terrified, Kleitos and his own charioteer looking bewildered. "Tell them what you told me," Sithon barked.

After hearing the man's suspicions about the wheels and the axle, Dryas's driver said, "You can't blame *me* if the chariot fell apart. I didn't make it happen. I only jumped off to save my life. If anyone is to blame, it's the man who was supposed to attach the wheels to the chariots. Why—"

"Search him," the king ordered, cutting short his excuses. In a moment, the pouch that Pallene had given the guard was found tucked into the charioteer's robe. People murmured as the king spilled a small heap of gold coins out of the pouch.

"That's—that's not mine," the driver babbled. "I was just holding it for a friend."

The king ignored him and turned to Kleitos, whose mouth gaped open in astonishment. "What do you know about this?"

"Who, me?" Kleitos looked even more confused than before.

"A charioteer wouldn't earn this much money in a lifetime," Sithon said. "Someone must have bribed Dryas's driver to take the pins out of the wheel to cause this accident. Who else but you would pay him to kill your rival?"

Kleitos had no answer. Pallene tried to speak, but her father hushed her.

"Take Kleitos to the altar and slit his throat," the king commanded.

Then a voice spoke from the crowd. It was Pallene's guard. "Kleitos had nothing to do with it," his deep voice boomed. "I was the one who paid Dryas's driver to loosen the pins that held the wheels to the axle. It's my fault Dryas died."

"And where did *you* get the money?" the king demanded. He knew how little he paid his servants. The guard fell silent, but the king saw him glance at Pallene.

The king turned to her in fury. "From *you?* From my first-born daughter, my favorite, the girl I loved so deeply that I fought off every man who tried to take her away from me?"

The guard tried to protest that the money was his, that Pallene had had nothing to do with the accident, but the king was too furious to listen. "Bring my older daughter to the funeral pyre," he ordered. "There I will sacrifice her to appease the shade of Dryas."

In vain did the guard protest that Pallene had not known what he was planning to do with her money. In vain did Rhoeteia beg for her sister's life. The king wouldn't listen. No matter who had paid the bribe, his daughter and her love for Kleitos had caused the death of a brave man. Both justice and the king's honor demanded her death in return.

Without another word, Sithon strode off to the beach, where dry wood had been piled high, ready to set alight. Dryas's pale, lifeless body lay on top of it.

Pallene shook off the hands of the men who tried to drag her to the pyre and walked toward it as serenely as if she were taking a stroll in the palace garden. She tried to calm her terror, despite the wailing and sobbing of her sister. "It will all be over soon," she told herself. When she saw her father, a grim expression on his face and a blazing torch in his hand, she hesitated. Then she swallowed, held her head high, and approached him.

But Pallene never reached the king. The heavens, which all day had been a lovely pure blue, darkened. The wind rose into a roar, and as the crowd scurried for shelter, rain fell so heavily that no one could see the person standing next to him.

The strange storm ended as suddenly as it had begun, and when the bewildered people moved out of their shelters, wringing out their soggy robes and slipping in the mud that just minutes before had been firm ground, they saw a woman standing in front of the pyre, which was, of course, soaked through. It would be impossible to light it for days. The woman was so lovely—and so dry—that everybody knew instantly that she was no mere mortal.

"I am Aphrodite, goddess of love," she informed them. "And if you are looking for someone to blame for this death, look no further than my own son, for it is due to him that Pallene and Kleitos fell in love. Put away your knife, Sithon, and give your daughter to this man. I myself will see to it that Dryas's shade rests easily in the realm of the dead." With those words, she disappeared.

Sithon was relieved that he wouldn't have to burn his daughter alive. He wasted no time in following the goddess's orders, and within a day, Pallene and Kleitos were married. Sithon died soon after, leaving Kleitos to rule, and Kleitos renamed both his country and its capital city Pallene in honor of his beloved wife.

I DO—BUT DO I HAVE TO?

Some ancient Greeks might not have been happy to marry the person their parents chose for them, but you never see anyone in ancient times saying that it's unfair that you can't marry for love. Being with the one you love wasn't the point of marriage. Choice of a spouse was a business and social matter—even, in the case of powerful families, a political matter. True, there are some stories from ancient Greece about loving couples, but being in love with your spouse was considered a lucky outcome, not something you could count on. Most couples who fell in love probably did so after the wedding, not before it.

BE CAREFUL WHAT YOU WISH FOR

Ah! Almost halfway through!

Wait—where are you going? Can't you stay a little longer? I'll try to be quick—I can't stand to be this close and not finish. If you have to be somewhere, can't you use that little thing you people always carry and tell them you'll be late?

Thanks. I appreciate it, I really do. That little thing you talk on is awfully handy, isn't it? So many misunderstandings that made problems in the myths could have been avoided if someone had been able to get in touch with people who were far away. If Kydippe had been able to call the plowman and tell him to bring the oxen back—but you don't know what I'm talking about, do you? Here's what happened.

Like I said before, some things never change, despite all your modern technology. For three thousand years, I've heard complaints that young people are spoiled, that they don't respect their elders, and that nowadays—whenever "nowadays" might be—everyone treats them as if they were more important than their parents. Maybe this is true and maybe it isn't, but people said it back in my time and probably before then, all the way back to the Golden Age. What do you think? You're young, but I'll bet you don't feel like everyone worships you, right?

Anyway, that's what this myth is about. Youth is supposed to be such a great time of life that—well, you'll see. I'll warn you that this tale has a sad ending, or at least that's how it would probably seem to you modern folk. A lot of the ancient Greeks would have thought it was a really happy ending. You can decide for yourself.

More than two thousand years ago, two teenage brothers named Kleobis and Biton lived in the proud and independent Greek city-state of Argos. The brothers were as proud and independent as their homeland. Like most people of the time, they were farmers. Their father was dead, and they lived with their mother. They weren't rich, but they were comfortable enough. Their mother, Kydippe (not the same Kydippe who was tricked into marriage by Akontios), was a priestess in the service of Hera, queen of the gods.

When it came time for Hera's festival, Kydippe was eager to go to her great temple, the Heraion, to help with the celebration. She got dressed and made up with great care, since a priestess's beauty honors the goddess. The white makeup that covered Kydippe's face made her look like a lady of leisure who never had to work in the fields, and bright rouge made from crushed berries reddened her cheeks and lips. A servant darkened her eyelashes and eyebrows with charcoal, joining the line of her brows over the bridge of her nose, and carefully painted sacred designs on her cheeks with a slim brush. Another servant bound her hair into an intricate knot at the back of her head. Dressed in a tunic of the finest linen, Kydippe wore ornaments of gold and jewels in her hair, around her neck and wrists and ankles, and on her fingers.

"You're as beautiful as the goddess herself," Biton told her.

"I'll go harness the oxen to the wagon," Kleobis offered. He went to the barn but came back almost immediately.

"The oxen haven't returned from the field yet," he said. "But don't worry, Mother. Surely they'll be here soon."

At first, Kydippe wasn't concerned. True, the temple was five miles away and the oxen had been plowing all morning, but they were powerful. They had enough strength to get Kydippe to the Heraion in plenty of time to participate in the sacrifice and the other rituals planned for that day.

But time passed, and the oxen didn't appear. Both boys went out to look for them, but the fields were large and the oxen were nowhere to be seen. The priestess paced up and down, worry spreading across her face.

Her sons drew aside to confer. "Do you think she can walk all the way to the temple?" Kleobis asked.

Biton shook his head. "Not dressed in her finery." They imagined their mother's face streaked with sweat, making her eyeliner run and her reddened cheeks smudge. The other priestesses would be appalled, and Kydippe would be mortified. Besides, it would be dishonorable for a priestess to arrive on foot like a common person.

Kleobis looked at the wagon. He knew the disappointment his mother must feel at the prospect of missing the festival. Even worse would be her fear that failing to show up would anger Hera, the powerful goddess-queen. No, he couldn't allow that. He glanced at Biton and saw from his brother's eyes that he too was determined to get Kydippe to the festival on time.

There was only one thing to do. The boys hitched themselves to the wagon and leaned hard into the yoke. At first the wheels refused to turn, but then slowly, slowly, the brothers were able to move down the drive, until they came to a stop in front of their mother.

"Boys, you can't pull me all the way there!" Kydippe exclaimed.

"Of course we can," Biton said.

"Climb in, Mother," Kleobis added. "You don't want them to start without you!"

A servant helped Kydippe, still protesting, into the wagon, and she settled onto the seat. She had no need to use the reins or whip, of course. Kleobis and Biton pulled her over the dusty road in the hot sun, over pebbles and rocks that scraped their sandaled feet, until they reached the Heraion.

The priestesses were just about to go ahead with the ceremony, even with one of their number missing. Only once their mother had been safely escorted to the sacred area did Kleobis and Biton allow themselves to be unhitched from the wagon and take a drink of water. As the sacrifices and prayers began, everyone exclaimed at their strength, and even more, at their love for their mother and their piety.

When all the rituals had been performed and the feast had ended, the worshippers settled down in the temple for the night. Kydippe looked at her two boys, deep in exhausted sleep. They were so handsome, so young, so full of strength, and so dutiful. Everyone admired what they had done, and other women were already telling their own sons to be as good and as pious as Kleobis and Biton.

Quietly, Kydippe stood before the altar of the goddess and said a prayer from her full heart: "Dearest Hera, goddess-queen, ruler of the heavens, you too are a mother. You know how I love these boys, and how they have honored both you and me by what they did today.

"Please, Hera, give my sons the greatest gift a mortal can receive. I don't know what that gift might be. I leave it to you to reward them suitably."

The next morning, the plowman who worked for them led the oxen to the temple. He apologized for losing track of the time the day before and hitched the oxen to the wagon. After Kydippe had been helped aboard, she sent the plowman to wake her sons. They must be tired and sore, their feet cut and bruised. They would ride, too; the strong beasts wouldn't notice their weight.

But when the plowman ran back from the temple, his face was as white as Kydippe's had been during the ceremony. "Your s-s-sons," he stammered. "Your sons, my lady—they won't wake up!"

And they never did. The goddess had granted their mother's wish as only an immortal being who doesn't understand death could grant it: Kleobis and Biton had died when they were young and beautiful and admired by all. They never had to know shame or illness or old age.

Did Kydippe thank the goddess? Or did she curse her and refuse to worship her again? Herodotus, who was the first to write down this story, doesn't say.

THERE'S NO ACCOUNTING FOR TASTE

In ancient Greece, a unibrow was thought to make a woman look both intelligent and beautiful, and dark makeup was often used to connect her eyebrows.

ARGOS LOVES HERA

The worship of Hera was particularly important in Argos. One of the names by which the queen of the gods was known was Ἥρα Ἀργεία (Argive Hera, or Hera of Argos), and the goddess once said, "The three cities I love best are Argos, Sparta, and Mycenae of the broad streets." Her great temple, the Heraion, which stood in Argos, held an enormous gold-and-ivory statue of the goddess. This spot was so important that it was where King Agamemnon was named the leader of the men of Argos in the run-up to the Trojan War.

DEATH IS FOREVER—OR IS IT?

Why are you getting up? Was that one too sad or something? Sorry about that, but life in ancient Greece was pretty tough. You're lucky that not many people die young these days, the way Kleobis and Biton did. I know, I know—some still do, and it's terribly sad, but your doctors can fix a lot of things that killed people in my time. They can't fix everything, though. Many mysteries remain, and who knows—maybe someday, a scientist will find a medicine like the magic herb in the story I'm about to tell you, something that will save as many lives as your antibiotics and vaccines do. Interested? Great.

You know, I've seen some scary-looking snakes in these woods. Sometimes they even go slithering over me, which would make me shiver if I could still shiver, and on hot days, they like to warm themselves in the sun on me. I'm not bothered by snakes, especially now that they can't bite me, but I don't like to feel them sliding around on my face.

Greece has only one kind of venomous snake: the adder, like the one that bit my poor Eurydice. So I think this story originally came from someplace other than Greece, maybe from Maionia, which is in the western part of what you people call Turkey. There are lots of snakes in Turkey, including one that has a hood like a cobra's and that sounds kind of like the monster in this story, about Tylos and the dragon.

Tylos was a young man who lived in Maionia with his sister, a tree nymph, or dryad, named Moria. In Maionia, there also lived a *drakon*—a hideous snake, or perhaps a dragon (the word δράκων can mean either one). This reptile, whatever it was, lived in a wild area, where it lay in wait for prey. Passersby, cows, even whole flocks of sheep would disappear down its huge throat. When it finished eating, it would blow out a great blast of air, and sometimes the blast would terrify someone nearby long enough for the snake to grab this victim, too.

One day, as Tylos strolled near a river with his sister, he accidentally brushed against the drakon, which instantly spread its hood and attacked him. Moria shrieked at the sight of this reptile with rows of teeth in its gaping jaw and a long, muscular body. The drakon didn't just bite the young man; it wrapped its tail around his neck and torso, and with its fangs, it ripped at his face, spitting poison all the while. Not surprisingly, Tylos fell dead from this lethal combination of poison, face ripping, and strangulation.

The drakon stayed on the youth's body, mauling Tylos even as he lay lifeless. The dryad must have been immune to the creature's attack, for she managed to pull the terrifying beast off her brother without being injured. The drakon hissed and spit at Moria as she saved her brother from being devoured.

Tylos's mutilated face and body were a horrible sight, and Moria wailed so loudly that a giant named Damasen heard her cries. Damasen was no ordinary giant, if you can call any giant ordinary. His mother was none other than Gaia, the earth, and he was born fully bearded and armed like a soldier, even holding a spear.

He approached Moria and asked, "Why are you crying?" but she was so distraught, she couldn't speak. She pointed wordlessly at the writhing reptile and at the corpse of her brother, lying in the dust.

Damasen didn't hesitate for a moment. He tore a tree from the ground and, wielding it like a club, ran toward the drakon.

The creature hissed a challenge and flung itself at the giant. The drakon was so huge, this caused the ground to tremble as though in an earthquake. It wrapped its long body around the giant's feet and spiraled up his body. Rolling its eyes and breathing its foul breath into his face, it opened its mouth and spat yellow, foamy poison into Damasen's eyes. Then it reared up over his head, looking for a spot unprotected by his armor, where it could sink its fangs.

But the monster was used to dealing with mere humans and sheep and cows, not with someone as large and strong and battle-proven as the son of the Earth, and it had met its match. Damasen shook the serpent off his arms and legs and whirled the tree in the air—once, twice, three times—and then smashed it down on the drakon, right where its head joined its long neck.

All was still. Moria was stunned into silence, and Damasen stood panting near the two dead bodies, Tylos's and the drakon's, wiping the stinking drakon spit off his face and recovering from the fight.

Then a slithery sound reached the ears of the girl and the giant, and out of the shrubs poked a narrow head. It looked around as if wondering what all the commotion was about. Then it spied the reptile's broken body, and the rest of the creature emerged.

It was another drakon—technically a *drakaina*, for it was a female. She coiled herself out of the dust, her long tail dragging behind her like the train of a gown, and headed straight for the drakon's body.

"What do you think she wants?" Moria whispered to Damasen. He could only shake his head.

Moria was terrified. Would the creature realize that Damasen had killed her mate and attack the giant, too? Would she tear at Moria the way the drakon had torn at Tylos?

But neither the girl nor the giant could have imagined the strange thing the drakaina did next. After nosing the drakon's corpse and realizing her mate was dead, she turned and wound with great haste through the rocks that lay around them, toward a hill covered with flowers and herbs. Moria and Damasen watched in amazement as the creature yanked a plant known as the flower of Zeus from the ground and, clutching it in her teeth, came slithering back. She coiled herself next to the drakon and carefully dropped the plant against one of its nostrils.

For a moment, nothing happened. Then the drakon's body gave a great shudder, and bit by bit, as life returned first to one part of the monster and then to another, the creature moved. His tail was the last to revive. Finally, cold breath hissed out of his many-toothed mouth.

Moria clutched at Damasen, afraid that the two creatures would come at them. But the drakon had learned his lesson, and with his mate, he went slithering back into his den rather than daring to approach the giant again.

DRAGONS

The noun δράκων comes from the verb δέρκεσθαι (derkesthai), meaning "to see clearly." Many snakes have poor eyesight, though.

A TOUGH BABY

The Cretan goddess of childbirth gave Damasen a shield on his first day of life, and the goddess of strife and discord was his nanny. His name means "the subduer."

Moria wasted no time. She picked up the flower of Zeus and laid it against her Tylos's nostril. Then she waited.

At first, she thought the flower must work only on monsters, because her brother lay as pale and motionless as before. Just as she was about to give up and begin preparations for Tylos's funeral, she thought she saw a faint color come to his torn cheek. Then one foot twitched, and he raised his head and blinked. Slowly and shakily, he stood. He looked around, bewildered, and then he raised his hands to the gods in thanks as the blood flowed back through him.

Tylos lived for a long time after that, but on his face and body, he always carried the deep scars that the drakon had inflicted on him.

YOU ONLY LIVE TWICE

I'm running out of ideas! Let's see...the last story was about coming back to life. How about something similar for number eleven—about a guy who was born twice. Does that sound too strange?

I have to admit that once you really look at them, some of the stories my people told don't make a lot of sense. Sometimes that's because the Greeks were great travelers; they went to a lot of different lands, and when they got home, they'd tell the stories they'd heard. If they didn't really understand what was going on, they'd make up something to explain whatever it was they didn't get.

Once in a while, a tale they brought home had something in common with a story already known in Greece, and the two got mixed together. That's why you'll read a myth that says someone's mother is a particular goddess, and in another version, the mother is someone else. Or someone will die in one myth, but in another one, that person is still alive a long time later. These contradictions didn't seem to bother anyone in my day, and I don't see why they should bother anyone now.

That kind of confusion looks like what happened with the tale of Zagreus, which might have come from Turkey. It got mixed up with a myth about Dionysos, the Greek god of wine. Sometimes you hear that Zagreus and Dionysos are the same god with two different names; other times, they're two separate gods. You can believe whichever version you want. Or neither one.

Anyway, Zagreus, according to the blended myth, was the son of Zeus, king of the gods. His mother was Persephone, the goddess of the underworld. Given this parentage, you'd think Zagreus would be no ordinary baby, and you'd be right. He was born with horns on his head, and when he was just a few hours old, he climbed onto a tiny throne and grasped miniature thunderbolts, a gift from his proud father, in his pudgy hand.

Zeus declared that this son would be his heir, although it's hard to imagine what he would need with an heir. Zeus is immortal—what's the point of being his heir if he's never going to die? See what I mean about the myths not always making sense?

Sorry, back to the story. In any event, it's an honor to be declared someone's heir, and Zeus's wife, Hera, became enraged at this insult to Ares, her own son with Zeus.

"I've just about had it with my husband!" Hera declared. "It's bad enough that he sneaks around chasing one girl after another, but when he puts their children above mine, well, that's going too far."

She made up her mind to get rid of the baby. Zeus was well aware of his wife's jealousy, so he summoned a gang of spirits of the wilderness, the Kouretes, to guard the child. These wild spirits performed ferocious dances around Zagreus's throne, brandishing their weapons to scare off anyone who might try to harm him. Whenever he cried, they clashed their shields and spears together so that no one, especially Hera, would hear him.

To keep his son content to stay put and not go wandering into danger, Zeus gave him lovely toys: a spinning top, a ball that returned on its own to the hand that had thrown it, dolls with moving legs and arms so cunningly crafted that the little god thought he was playing with living beings. Nymphs brought him golden apples, and many others gave presents to the little god who was supposed to rule them one day.

Hera soon figured out where the baby was. She knew that the Kouretes would never allow her to get close to the infant, but, determined to cause him harm, she summoned a group of Titans. These gigantic sons of the earth goddess, Gaia, had once ruled over the world and even the other immortals. Years earlier, Zeus had sent some of the Titans to dwell in the deepest pit of the underworld so that he could take over as ruler. Understandably, the whole tribe had resented him ever since. Hera knew they would be more than happy to help her out.

"I need you to do something for me," Hera said to the four Titans who obeyed her call. They looked at one another, not knowing whether to trust the wife of their greatest enemy. Most of the Titans were not terribly intelligent, but they knew enough to be wary. "My husband has a new son, and he dotes on the child. I want you to get rid of him. I don't care how you do it. Just do it." These words set their dull minds at ease, since the Titans were eager to make Zeus pay for taking their power away from them.

Hera departed, leaving them to make a plan. Despite the dim wits of these four, Titans in general were clever craftsmen. After all, the Titan Prometheus had created humans, as well as many of the powerful spirits called *daimones*, and his brother Epimetheus had made all the marvelous variety of animals. Working together, the Titans came up with a wonderful new toy for Zagreus—so marvelous, they figured it would distract even the guardian Kouretes, and the Titans would have their chance to do what the queen of the gods had ordered.

Now, how to get close enough to the baby to give him their gift? Luckily for the Titans, the Kouretes weren't any brighter than they were. All the Titans had to do to disguise themselves was to rub chalk over their hands and faces. When they walked in carrying something wrapped in brightly colored cloth, the unsuspecting Kouretes put down their spears and bows and shields to see the gift these huge, strangely white men were bringing to the child in their care.

Little Zagreus eagerly tore the wrapping off his present. He held it up, and at first he was disappointed. It was only a circle of highly polished bronze with a handle—a simple mirror. He pouted as he looked at his own chubby face, at his dark eyes, at the small horns poking out from among his curls—and then he started. Instead of a round, dimpled face, what stared back at him from the mirror was a face with a long, hairy muzzle, eyes with square pupils, and a waggling beard. It looked like he had turned into a goat! His free hand flew to his cheek. To his astonishment, he felt his own face, while in the mirror, he still saw the goat's face, now with a cloven hoof caressing it. He was still the same; the only thing that had changed was his reflection.

As Zagreus watched, the goat face dissolved and his own reappeared, only to change again, this time into the golden, furry features of a lion cub. The baby pulled back his lips, and instead of toothless gums, long fangs glistened at him from the polished bronze. He laughed in delight, and the Kouretes gathered around to see and marvel. One of them snatched the mirror away, and they all clamored for a turn. None of them paid the least attention to the baby god, who was crying and reaching for his new toy.

The Titans didn't wait. Their leader picked up Zagreus, while the others drew out the knives they had concealed in their robes. From afar, Zeus saw what was happening and hurled a thunderbolt to stop the Titans, but it was too late. The giants quickly hacked Zagreus to bits. The Kouretes fled, terrified of what Zeus would do to them for failing to protect his son.

And the rage of the king of the gods was indeed terrifying. He went on a rampage, throwing so much lightning from Mount Olympos that the whole world—which was Gaia, the Titans' mother, remember—burst into flame. Mountains ran with snowmelt. Forests were destroyed, rivers boiled, cities fell. Still the king of the gods showed no mercy, and he continued to attack the earth.

Zeus didn't stop his ferocious assault until his daughter Athena appeared before him, holding something out to him. He paused in his furious attack long enough to take a look, and on her outstretched palm, he saw a small red heart, beating.

The heart had to belong to someone or something immortal, for no mortal heart can continue to beat outside its body. The king of the gods looked at Athena with sudden hope, and she nodded. "It's your son's heart," she said softly. "His mother snatched it from the flames and gave it to me to bring to you."

Zeus laid down his quiver and carefully carried his son's tiny heart to a princess with whom he had recently fallen in love. (He had already forgotten Zagreus's mother.) He inserted Zagreus's still-beating heart in her chest, and in a few months, the princess gave birth to the same baby boy, only this time, they named him Dionysos.

GAMES ANCIENT GREEKS PLAYED

Babies and children in ancient Greece played with many toys that are familiar today: dolls (some with jointed arms and legs), clay or wooden animals on wheels that could be pulled with a string, yo-yos, dice, balls (the balls didn't really bounce, so the Greeks mostly played catch and similar games with them), tops, hobbyhorses (a stick with a carved animal's head at one end), puppets, and wagons. They played games similar to tag, kick the can, rock-paper-scissors, jacks, capture the flag, spud, and basketball.

III.
GODS AND HUMANS

FROM MORTAL TO GODDESS

So according to the story I just told you, the god of wine, Dionysos, was born from the heart of a burned-up god named Zagreus. Zagreus's father was Zeus, king of the gods, and his mother was Persephone, queen of the dead.

In the myth that's coming up, Zagreus's father was still Zeus, but his mother was a human princess. According to this version, Dionysos wasn't born from the heart of Zagreus that was implanted in the chest of a princess, but from his own self implanted in his father's thigh. Clear? I didn't think so.

It's probably easier not to worry about where Dionysos came from or whether he was one god or two, and just listen to the story. If you've heard part of it, just be patient. Most of it is new—I hope. I'm running out of time. I really need to tell Eurydice how bad I feel for what I did. If you've ever had a fight with your best friend and they moved away before you could apologize, you know what I mean.

So Zeus was having a romance with a princess named Semele. When Zeus's wife, Hera, found out that Semele was going to have a baby, she became jealous, understandably. She convinced Semele to ask Zeus to prove that he was truly the king of the gods and ruler of the sky, as he had told her he was. Hera knew that challenging the proud lord of the immortals was risky. She hoped that Semele would be injured or killed if Zeus did what she asked, and Hera wouldn't have to take the blame for her death.

At first, Zeus said no, he wouldn't prove who he was— that if she really loved him, she'd take his word for it. But Semele was stubborn, and she became so insistent that he reluctantly agreed to appear to her in his true form. He tried to protect her from his immortal splendor, but even revealing himself only partially proved fatal: His glory was so brilliant that she burned to death.

Zeus saved the unborn Dionysos from his mother's ashes and sewed the tiny body into his own thigh until his son was ready to be born. Somehow, the baby turned out healthy, but the king of the gods still had a problem: what to do with his little son? How to keep him safe from the furious Hera? Zeus's mind turned to Semele's favorite sister, Ino. Semele had always said that Ino was kind and willing to help people.

Ino was married to a king named Athamas. He had a son and a daughter by his first wife, and he and Ino had two sons. So the household was already pretty full when a servant told Ino one day that a man carrying a baby had appeared at the door and had asked to see her. Ino hurried to see what the stranger wanted.

Ino was the daughter of a goddess, so she immediately recognized that the man standing in the sunshine with a sleeping baby in his arms, the wings on his cap and sandals fluttering in the breeze, was no mortal. He was far taller even than her royal husband, and a strange and beautiful light shone from his face. "I know you!" she exclaimed. "You're my cousin Hermes!"

The gods were all related to one another, though it took Ino and Hermes a little while to figure out exactly what their relationship was. Once that was established, Ino invited the messenger of the gods to have something to eat and drink. Servants brought out platters of bread and cheese and goblets of wine well diluted with water, as was the Greek custom.

"Let me hold the baby," Ino said, reaching for the little boy. Hermes passed her the tiny newborn, who immediately lunged for her goblet. "Goodness!" said Ino.

"I know," Hermes nodded, munching on a piece of bread. "He's already crazy for wine."

This was odd, but Ino forgot about it when Hermes explained the predicament that Zeus found himself in, with his furious wife wanting to kill his child. He concluded by saying, "So he wants you to raise the baby."

Much as Ino wanted to help her dead sister's son, she hesitated. She already had two stepchildren who were older than her own sons, which threatened any inheritance her boys might get from their father. And if they welcomed Zeus's child into their family, what would that mean for her darling boys? On the other hand, it was hard—actually, it was impossible—to say no to the king of the gods. Besides, with his dimples and his curls, her nephew was so cute that she hated the thought of any harm coming to him. So she agreed and Hermes left, twirling his sandals on his toes as he flew off, relieved to be free of the child so hated by Hera.

When King Athamas returned home, he was astonished to see a baby in a cradle in their bedroom. Ino closed the door hurriedly and explained the situation. "We'll pretend he's a girl, to throw Hera off the track," she said. "You know she has spies everywhere, and they'll be looking for a little boy. We'll keep him hidden indoors until he's old enough to take care of himself. Zeus will be very grateful, I'm sure."

Athamas reluctantly agreed to his wife's plan, and for a while, it looked as though they had fooled the queen of the gods. But somehow she discovered that Semele's child had not only survived but was growing up safe and sound in the luxurious palace of a king. Hera was enraged. Putting aside her hatred of Dionysos for the time being, she turned her rage on Athamas and Ino. She decided to give them the worst punishment a parent can endure.

Hera threw a spell down from Mount Olympos, turning both Athamas and Ino insane. In her madness, Ino thought her older son was attacking her, so in terror, she killed him. Horrified, Athamas commanded his own son, "Kill your stepmother!" But before the boy could act, Dionysos, grateful to his aunt for saving his life, cast a cloak of darkness around her, which hid her from both her stepson and her maddened husband.

When Ino's mind cleared, she recognized the danger she was in. She snatched up her younger boy, Melikertes, and sped across the white plain. She ran hard and fast, white dust clinging to her feet as she fled her husband's murderous rage. But Athamas followed close behind, and since she was carrying the heavy boy, he quickly started gaining on her.

Ino looked around desperately and saw no escape. Athamas would seize her, and in his insanity and fury, who knew what he would do?

She realized that she was heading straight for the edge of a cliff, high above a sea full of crashing waves and leaping dolphins. Without stopping to think, she clutched her son tight and threw herself into the air, calling on the gods to help her.

Still holding Melikertes, Ino plunged deep into the water. She kicked desperately, trying to rise to the surface, but it was no use. She wondered frantically how long her son would manage to hold his breath, but when she looked down at his dear little face, she saw that he was smiling at her. He even seemed to be breathing. How could that be?

At that moment, her own air ran out and she gasped, terrified at the thought of the cold water rushing into her lungs. But to her astonishment, she found that she could breathe easily. She felt better than she had in years, and Melikertes looked perfectly happy and healthy. A god had heard her plea—not Zeus, who was too afraid of his wife to save her, but Poseidon, Ino's great-grandfather, who ruled the sea. He had turned her into a sea goddess.

From that time on, Ino was known as Leukothea, the White Goddess, since she had fallen into the ocean covered in white dust. Ever after, Leukothea came to the aid of drowning people, most famously the lost sailor Odysseus, to whom she gave a magic scarf that helped him reach shore after a disastrous shipwreck. Melikertes also had a new name: Palaimon, the Wrestler. He inherited his mother's loving nature and desire to help others. He became the god who took care of ships as they entered a harbor, always a treacherous part of a sea voyage.

PHRIXOS AND HELLE

Ino wasn't always kind and loving to children. In one myth, she hated her two stepchildren (Athamas's son Phrixos and his daughter Helle). To get rid of them, she secretly roasted all the wheat that was to be used for seed the following spring. The farmers didn't know that the seed had been ruined, so they sowed it in their fields. When the crops failed to grow, Ino bribed her servants to say that an oracle had declared that Phrixos had to be sacrificed to save the people from starvation. Phrixos and his sister escaped on the back of a magical flying ram. Helle fell off and drowned, but Phrixos made it to the land of Kolkhis. When the ram died, Phrixos gave its beautiful golden fleece to the Kolkhian king. Much later, the hero Jason stole the Golden Fleece during an adventure-filled journey with his sailors, the Argonauts.

AN OREAD SCORNED

It's possible that you've heard of Paris, one of the princes of Troy. Whether or not you know who he was, I'm pretty sure this story will be new to you. I hope so, anyway. The sun is close to setting, and I still have—let me see—five stories left. I'd better get started if I want to see Eurydice again. I can't believe how stupid I—never mind. I said I wouldn't talk about that again.

But I really was stupid.

Paris, as you may know, was one of the many sons of King Priam of Troy. He didn't grow up in the palace, though, with the rest of the royal family. Instead, he lived as a simple shepherd, unaware of his true identity. And his parents were unaware that he was alive. In fact, his father was sure he was dead, since he had ordered his newborn son's death. I know, there's lots of baby-killing in these stories, right? But things usually turn out fine for the mythical babies. See if you think things turn out well here.

Paris's father had ordered a shepherd to kill his son because not one but *two* prophecies had said that the royal baby would cause the fall of the kingdom of Troy. The shepherd obeyed, and left the baby on the slopes of Mount Ida. He felt terrible about what he had done, so a few days later, he went back to retrieve what he was sure would be a tiny dead body. At least, he thought, he could give the little prince a decent burial.

To his astonishment, the shepherd found the baby alive and well, since a bear had found him and was raising him along with her cubs. The shepherd was ashamed that he had obeyed the king; he had been more heartless than a ferocious bear, since she had saved the child. He took Paris home with him and raised him as his own son. He never told him about his true beginnings.

But it was only a matter of time before Fate figured out that the prince of Troy was still alive and where he was living.

One day after he had grown up, Paris was wandering near a river in the foothills of Mount Ida when he heard singing. The voice was so lovely that he crept forward, not wanting to disturb the singer, until he saw a pretty young woman sitting on a rock. She sang as she dangled her feet in the river and combed out her long, dark hair, which was wet from a swim.

The woman must have sensed that someone was staring at her, because she turned and looked at Paris. Even though he was a stranger, she didn't seem afraid. "Are you lost, shepherd?" she called to him.

In ancient Greece, respectable women usually avoided strange men, so Paris was surprised that she didn't flee. Approaching her cautiously, he saw that she was even more beautiful than she had appeared from a distance. "No, I'm not lost," he said. "I'm just taking a walk."

She recognized his discomfort and guessed its cause. "Don't worry; it's perfectly proper for us to talk," she assured him. "We're in the presence of my father."

Paris looked around, but he didn't see anyone. Then he jumped back as the water at the woman's feet surged, and a tall gray-green man reared up out of it. His long hair looked like the coarse grass that grew on the riverbank, and fish wriggled out of his beard and plopped into the ripples. He glared a warning at Paris, then sank back into the water.

This was no mere woman he was talking with, Paris realized, but a mountain nymph—an oread—and the daughter of the spirit of the river. No wonder she wasn't afraid of him.

Under her father's watchful eye, Paris sat on a rock next to the oread, whose name was Oinone, and from that day on, he went back to the river to visit her whenever he could. Soon he and Oinone fell in love. Paris was surprised when she agreed to marry him, a mere mortal and a humble shepherd.

After they were married, Oinone revealed that she knew there was more to Paris than he or anyone else suspected. "I have the gift of prophecy," she informed him. "I can foretell the future, and I also see things that other people don't. One thing I know that even you are ignorant of is that you are a prince, the son of King Priam of Troy."

"No!" he exclaimed. "That's impossible!" But she insisted, and so he asked the shepherd, the man he had always thought was his father, about his parentage.

The shepherd confirmed what Oinone had said. When Paris told Oinone that he'd learned she was right, she didn't seem surprised. But when he said that he was going to the palace to claim his rightful place as the prince (or at least one of them; King Priam had about a hundred sons and daughters), she begged him not to go.

"I can't leave here. I'm an oread, a mountain nymph, remember? I can't live in a palace. If you go to Troy and live with the king—and remember, he's the man who ordered you to be killed!—you'll have to leave me here alone. Besides, if the gods know you're the prince, they'll take notice of you. Then the fate that was foretold, that you will destroy your father's land, will catch up with you. If you live here quietly with me, maybe you can escape it."

Paris was so in love with Oinone that he returned to his peaceful life, tending sheep. He participated in the games that herdsmen played in those days, one of which was to see whose bull was the best fighter. Paris offered a gold crown to anyone whose beast could defeat his. Soon, men from the surrounding countryside were bringing their bulls to Mount Ida and testing them against Paris's champion. But Paris's bull beat all the others.

It didn't take long for news of this powerful animal to reach the home of the gods, on Mount Olympos. Ares, the god of war, possessed an enormous bull that had never been beaten in a match. Disguising himself as a human herdsman, Ares pitted this bull against Paris's, and for the first time, the champion was defeated.

Without hesitation, Paris strode over to Ares, still unaware that he was a god, and placed the gold crown on his head. "Behold the winner!" he cried, and ordered a banquet to celebrate his rival's victory.

The gods had been watching the contest, and when Paris behaved so honestly and decently, they took notice. They asked one another, "Who *is* this guy? Where did he come from?"

If only Paris had whined that Ares had cheated, that his own bull was really the winner, he might have remained unnoticed. He and Oinone might have lived the rest of their days on sunny Mount Ida, tending their flocks, perhaps raising a houseful of children. But if there's anything Greek myths have to tell us, it's that no one can escape Fate.

Paris allowed himself to forget what his wife had told him, and in time, he and Oinone had a son they named Korythos. They lived happily, until Paris came home one evening and found his wife in tears.

Paris took her in his arms. "Tell me what's wrong," he said.

For a long time, she refused to answer, despite his coaxing. Finally, she said, "You're going to leave me."

"What?" He was astonished. "You know I love you more than anything else on earth!"

"Oh, I know that. And I love you. But that's just today. I foresee a time when you'll leave me for another woman, a queen who lives in a distant kingdom."

Paris protested and tried to reassure his wife that this would never happen, but she wouldn't cheer up. She said, "When you bring this foreign woman home, something terrible will happen. I can't be sure what, but it looks like a long and bloody war."

Paris fell silent, remembering that his father, King Priam of Troy, had tried to have him killed at birth because of the prophecies that he would someday bring ruin on his city. The first prophecy had come from his own mother: While pregnant with him, she had dreamed she gave birth to a flaming torch, which destroyed the high-walled city of Troy. The second prophecy came from Paris's half-brother, a seer who warned that a child born on a certain day would bring doom to Troy. Paris had been born just before nightfall on that very day.

Paris realized that Oinone was looking at him, probably wondering why her husband was so quiet. He took her hand. "My darling, please don't worry yourself over this. It will never happen."

"I hope you're right." She didn't sound very hopeful. "There's just one thing I want you to promise me."

"That I won't run off with this imaginary woman?"

"No, that's not it. I see that you're going to be terribly wounded in the war that will follow—by an arrow, I think. And when that happens, I want you to come to me. Apollo himself, the god of healing, taught me a lot about medicine. I know I'm the only one who will be able to heal you. Please swear that when that day comes, you'll allow me to do that."

Paris kissed her and promised, just to keep her happy, never thinking that any of this would happen.

But it did. One day, three goddesses were debating which of them was the most beautiful, and they decided that Paris should judge the beauty contest. After all, he was known to be fair; he had declared someone else's bull was stronger than his own, when most men would have cheated and claimed they had won. But Aphrodite, goddess of love, promised to give Paris Queen Helen of Sparta, the most beautiful woman in the world, if he named her the winner. Paris was so excited by this offer, he forgot all about judging fairly—as well as about his wife—and chose Aphrodite.

With that action, Paris's fate, and that of his city, was sealed. He traveled to Sparta, fell in love with Queen Helen, and took her home with him to Troy. In an effort to reclaim his wife, the king of Sparta gathered all his allies and attacked Troy. The war dragged on for years, and many men and some women and children on both sides died.

Finally, Paris was wounded, just as Oinone had foretold. The wound didn't appear serious at first, but the arrow that had injured him was poisoned, and soon it appeared he would die. He called his soldiers to him and ordered them to carry him to his old home, on Mount Ida.

As Paris rode home on his litter, he passed many places dear to him. There was the spot where his foster father had first abandoned him and then found him alive. There was the simple shepherd's hut in which he had grown up, and there was the river where he had met Oinone. The soldiers carried him through the pasture where he had put the winner's crown on Ares for having the best fighting bull in the world. Next he saw the field where he had played with his little boy, Korythos. Tears ran down Paris's face as he bitterly regretted leaving all this to run away with another man's wife.

He still hadn't composed himself when the litter passed through the front gates of his home. A handsome youth was practicing with his sword in the courtyard, and he stared at this pale man with wet cheeks, his face drawn in pain, his swollen ankle propped up on a cushion as he was carried into the house. This youth was Korythos. He had been only a toddler when Paris had left, and after so much time apart, they didn't recognize each other.

Oinone had foreseen Paris's arrival and was waiting for him in the front room of their house. Beads of sweat gathered on his forehead as the pain of the arrow's venom gripped him. He was unable to speak. He extended a hand to her, his eyes pleading.

Oinone looked at him, and her heart was torn. Paris was her husband. Once she had loved him so much, she had left everything dear to her—the fields and streams, the river that her father protected, her beloved mountain—and moved into this house to be with him. She still loved him.

But he had left her without a word to take up with another woman. She had heard that they'd had children together. When Helen's husband came to reclaim her, Paris fought for years to keep her. He had made a fool out of Oinone. Worse, he had left her alone to comfort their son, who didn't understand why his father had suddenly disappeared.

Oinone addressed the men carrying the litter. "There's nothing I can do," she said brusquely. "Take him away." And she turned her back on them, weeping silently. Feebly, Paris called her name, but she pretended not to hear him, although the pain in his voice broke her heart.

"Who was that man?" Korythos had come in and was looking at her, the practice sword dangling from his hand.

She didn't know how to answer him. My husband? Your father? The man who betrayed me and abandoned us? The man I love?

Suddenly, she snatched up the pouch of healing herbs that Apollo had given her and ran out the door and down the mountain path. "Wait!" she called. "Wait! I forgive you! I'll heal your wound!"

But she was too late. As she reached the shore of the river, she saw a plume of smoke rising, and she realized that it was Paris's funeral pyre. With an agonized cry, she threw herself onto the fire and burned to death.

After the flames died down, the mourners gathered the ashes that had been Paris and the ashes that had been Oinone and buried them in separate urns. They placed a column over each. But they set them up in such a way that it looked as though they faced away from each other.

Even in death, Paris and Oinone were united, yet apart.

A FEW (REALLY; THERE ARE LOTS MORE) NYMPHS AND WHAT THEY'RE ASSOCIATED WITH

alseid: sacred groves

anthousa: flowers

aura: breezes

dryad: forests

epimeliad: flocks of sheep and goats

hamadryad: oak and poplar trees

lampas: underworld

leimakis: meadows

limniad: lakes, marshes, swamps

naiad: fresh water

napaea: valleys

nereid: Mediterranean Sea

oceanid: oceans

oread or oreiad: mountains

potameid: rivers

THAT WOULD BE LIKE
NAMING YOUR BABY "CARSEAT"

When the shepherd found the infant Paris alive and well on Mount Ida, he carried the child home in a pouch. The ancient Greek word for "pouch" is πήρα, or *pera*, and this supposedly gave the child his name, Πάρις, or Paris.

OOPS

One story says that Oinone sent Korythos to Troy to try to convince Paris to return home, but Paris didn't recognize his own son and killed him.

IV.
CREATURES YOU NEVER KNEW ABOUT

THE HURRICANE HOUND
AND THE TEUMESSIAN FOX

Oh, that story makes me sad. If only Paris had kept pleading
with Oinone to forgive him, maybe she would have changed
her mind. I know that if I'm ever permitted to see Eurydice
again, I'll beg and beg her to forgive me for my—but never
mind. Time is running out, so here's a short myth that isn't
at all sad—not unless you're the dog or the fox in the story,
I guess. And even then, it could be worse.

There once was a hound whose name, Lailaps, means
"hurricane." Lailaps always caught what he hunted. This
isn't just because he was a great hunter, although he was.
He was also magical; some say he was even immortal. He
first appeared to guard the infant god Zeus, who was hiding from his father in a cave on the island of Crete. (Zeus's
father wanted to eat him, but that's another story.) This
great dog was passed down from owner to owner until he
wound up with a man named Kephalos, though some claim
the dog was a gift from Artemis, goddess of the hunt, to
Kephalos.

Anyway, one day Kephalos heard about a huge fox
that the gods had sent to the city of Teumessos to punish
its citizens for something; it's not clear exactly what the
crime was. Just as Lailaps was no ordinary dog, this was no

ordinary fox. She was the daughter of a monster called the Echidna, which was half human and half snake.

Just as Lailaps always caught his quarry, the Teumessian fox could never *be* caught. She escaped from every trap and eluded every dog that chased her. Once, some men surrounded her with nets, sure they'd finally gotten her, but the great fox leaped over the nets and escaped into the woods. She was so bold that she even ventured into town to eat people. The only way the people of Teumessos could cut down on her attacks was to feed her a child every month. Naturally, this made them very unhappy, but what else could they do?

Kephalos went to Teumessos with his dog and his spear to try to help. As soon as Lailaps caught the fox's scent, he lunged against his leash, eager to go after her. When Kephalos released him, Lailaps took off like an arrow shot from a bow. He chased the fox across plains, through forests, up hills, and down valleys. Kephalos climbed a hill to watch the pursuit.

The dog nearly caught the fox several times, but each time, she managed to escape. She sped away and then doubled back, circling as Lailaps's teeth snapped. The hound was never more than one pace behind her, but with each bite, he just missed her. Kephalos was afraid his magic hound would run himself to death.

Kephalos wasn't the only one watching this strange hunt; in their home on tall Mount Olympos, the gods were observing it, too. Zeus recognized his old friend Lailaps, the hound that had kept him safe when he was a baby. "How will this ever end?" the gods asked one another. "If the dog always catches his prey but the fox can never be caught, will the dog chase the fox forever?"

They turned to Zeus, sitting on his throne, his mighty brow furrowed. The situation irritated him: How could mere humans set up a situation that would last forever? Eternity was the privilege of the gods, not mortals! And besides, he hated to see his faithful guard-dog trapped in an endless chase.

Zeus made up his mind. He drew back his arm and hurled a spell toward earth.

Meanwhile, Kephalos had decided to use his magic spear that never missed its mark. Surely the dog and the spear together would be enough to stop the giant fox. He tossed it in his hand a few times to get its balance; then he too drew back his arm.

But unlike Zeus, Kephalos lowered his arm without throwing his weapon. Down in the field, he now saw not one fierce animal in hot pursuit of another, but two marble statues caught in mid-stride. In front was the huge fox, and right behind it, jaws open but destined never to snap shut, was Lailaps. Zeus had turned them both into stone.

Some, however, say that instead of turning them into statues, Zeus set Lailaps and the fox in the heavens as the constellations Canis Major and Canis Minor, where for eternity the Hurricane Hound chases the Teumessian Fox across the night sky.

LET'S JUST CALL HIM FIDO

Some wealthy Greeks kept dogs as pets, but most were probably used in hunting. Their names often showed their characters, or what their owners hoped their characters would be: Horme (Eager), Hormenos (Impulse), Methepon (Pursuer), Egertes (Vigilant), Korax (Raven), Marpsas (Seizer/Holder), Labros (Fierce), Eubolous (Shooter), Aello (Whirlwind), and Arkas (Bear). The athlete Atalanta called her dog by the gentler name of Aura (Breeze).

The vicious three-headed dog who guarded the underworld was named Cerberus (Κέρβερος in Greek). You'd think that this name would mean something ferocious, but actually, it probably means "Spot."

THE BRONZE MAN OF CRETE

I keep thinking of stories that I'll bet you already know, which won't do me any good. I'm so close, yet so far. I need to calm down so I can think.

I know—how about something from Crete? Many Greeks even in my day didn't know many Cretan myths. That's because in ancient times, the island of Crete wasn't part of Greece, the way it is today. It had a different culture, language, religion, and customs. I'm from Thrace, which is now a province of Greece, and Crete was almost as foreign to me as it probably is to you.

The little I know about Crete I learned from Greek travelers who went there and reported what they had seen, a lot of which they misunderstood. Sometimes they even outright lied about the Cretans, because the Cretans were the enemies of most of the people in Greece, and they thought it was funny to tell stories that made the Cretans look stupid or savage.

Here's an example. The Cretan sun god was a bull. (I know that sounds strange, but in a lot of ancient religions, the gods took the shape of animals. In fact, the Greeks' humanlike gods were unusual in those days.) There were probably some religious ceremonies on Crete where a priest of the sun god would wear a bull's-head mask. Maybe one of those ceremonies was a kind of pretend marriage between the sun god and a priestess of the moon goddess. It's possible that a person or two was sacrificed at this ceremony.

So say you were an ancient Greek tourist watching this ritual. The lighting was probably dim in the temple, and the air was smoky from all the torches. You might get confused and think that what you saw was a real wedding between a for-real half-man, half-bull monster and the moon goddess herself. And if the Cretans really did perform a human sacrifice, you'd find that pretty shocking.

When you got home to Greece, you'd have forgotten some of what you saw and mixed up most of the rest. You might even exaggerate what you saw when you told people about it, because it was so strange and frightening.

Something like this could be where the myth of the Minotaur came from. You know the Minotaur? The Greeks described him as half man, half bull. They said his father was King Minos of Crete and his mother was the priestess of the moon, and that he ate people. That's probably not really what the Cretans had in mind with their sun-worship ceremony, but you can see how Greek visitors might get confused.

Another story that the Greeks brought home from Crete is the tale of Talos. Like the story of the Minotaur, it's gotten all mixed up, and it's hard to know exactly what the Cretans believed about him—or *it*. Talos was a kind of robot made of bronze. He (or it) was shaped like a man (or maybe a bull. See? The myth is all mixed up), and he was alive. Well, maybe not alive, but he could move; in fact, he ran around the entire island of Crete three times a day. This wasn't easy, since Crete is pretty big; by your modern measurements, it's 649 miles around.

Some say that Talos was the son of the island of Crete and the sun god, and that he was the father of both the god of the forge, Hephaistos, and the queen of Crete. Others say that far from being the father of Hephaistos, he was actually *created* by Hephaistos. Others say that Talos was the sun god himself. Still others say that he was the last of the men of the Age of Bronze, a time when all humans were made of bronze and were huge and heroic. He's sometimes pictured with wings, sometimes not. Mixed-up enough for you?

One odd thing about Talos, which most of the versions agree on, was that he had only one vein in his body, but it didn't carry blood. Instead, it held a liquid called ichor—the same fluid that ran through the veins of the gods. A bronze nail in his heel kept the ichor from leaking out.

But enough about the contradictions and the weirdness. Let's get to the story.

The reason Talos ran around Crete three times a day was to guard the island from an attack by sea. If enemies approached, he threw huge boulders at them. If they managed to land anyway, he would build a fire and heat himself red-hot—remember, he was made of metal—and then he would embrace the invaders, and they would die in excruciating pain.

The story goes that one day, a foreign ship came sailing up to Crete. The ship was named the *Argo*, and its sailors were called Argonauts. (I was an Argonaut; did I tell you? I was there that day, and I remember it well.) The captain of the *Argo* was a Greek hero named Jason. He was sailing home with the hide of a magical flying ram, the Golden Fleece, which he had stolen from the land of Kolkhis.

After rowing for days in the hot sun, the Argonauts were desperately thirsty. As the ship approached the island, Jason saw a huge shining figure standing on the shore, brandishing a boulder in his enormous hand. "We just want to get some water!" Jason called to the giant. "Let us refill our barrels, and we'll be on our way." Talos didn't believe him—or maybe he didn't understand Greek (the Cretan language was totally different), or maybe he didn't care if the Argonauts died—and he tossed the boulder. It nearly landed on the *Argo*'s deck. The oarsmen hastily reverse-rowed until they were out of range, and then they tried to figure out what to do. They had to think fast. If they didn't get water soon, they would die.

Unfortunately for Talos, one of the passengers on the *Argo* was a woman named Medea, who had helped Jason steal the Golden Fleece. Later Greeks called her a witch, but she was probably a powerful priestess of the religion of her homeland, Kolkhis.

"Are you giving up so easily?" Medea asked the Argonauts. "What cowards you are! I can deal with him. Row toward the island until we're just far enough away to keep from getting sunk by a rock." Jason said that this was too dangerous, but Medea insisted, and he finally ordered the oarsmen to do as she said, while she went below to prepare for the confrontation.

When Medea received the signal that they were in position, she climbed out onto the deck of the *Argo*. The Argonauts fell silent at the sight of her in her beautiful purple robe (purple dye was so expensive that it was reserved for ceremonial clothing). She drew the folds of her robe over the lower half of her face and said a spell through the purple cloth, summoning the ancient spirits of death.

The sailors didn't understand the sacred language that Medea used in her chant, nor did they see the hideous fanged spirits that flew to Talos at her bidding, but they could tell that something powerful was happening.

Talos, standing on the cliff holding a boulder high above his head, was bewildered. What was that little purple human doing? And why was he suddenly being bombarded with gruesome visions? He lowered the boulder and backed away from the spirits. As he did so, his ankle grazed the sharp edge of a rock, pulling out the nail that held in his precious bodily fluid.

As the ichor poured out of his vein, Talos's vision grew dim and his head spun. The strength fled from his limbs, and he crashed to the earth like a gigantic tree felled by a woodsman's axe.

And that was the end of the bronze man of Crete. We went ashore and filled our water barrels, and then the oarsmen rowed away as fast as they could.

ANCIENT TECH

The giant robot Talos is mythical, but the ancient Greeks really did make some extremely complex machines. At least one Greek created a steam engine—imagine how different the world would be if someone had thought to attach it to a ship or to a wheeled cart! Another supposedly made a model bird that actually flew. The most amazing ancient Greek machine found so far is a computer that historians today call the "Antikythera mechanism," named for the island near where it was discovered in a shipwreck. Probably built early in the first century BCE (some think even earlier), this complex system of gears predicted the motion of the planets, which was important in planning religious festivals.

JUST DON'T MAKE HER MAD

In the *Argonautica*, his book about Jason's travels, the Greek poet Apollonius of Rhodes described the scene between Medea and Talos like this: "She knelt in prayer and called on them with three songs and three prayers. She hardened her soul with their evil and bewitched Talos's eyes with her own and flung the phantoms of death at him in an ecstasy of fury."

YOU LOOK GREAT, BUT WHAT'S THAT SMELL?

Purple dye was expensive, because it was made from mucus excreted by a gland of the murex, a sea snail. The glands were boiled to make the dye, a very smelly process.

THE CRUSHERS

We're almost there! Just two more, and I'll be done, as long as the sun doesn't set first.

I wonder if Eurydice misses me. It's been three thousand years, after all. Only one way to find out—I have to think of more stories.

Let's see, there's been too much death lately. How about something funny, a story that shows someone tricking the gods? That way, even if I don't make it to the underworld today, at least I'll have a laugh.

The brothers Ephialtes (his name means "nightmare") and Otos ("doom") were sons of Poseidon, the god of the sea. They were called the Aloadae—the Crushers—and they were huge. When they were nine years old, they were already twenty-seven cubits tall, which is about forty feet in your measurements, and they kept on growing.

One day, the Aloadae appeared before the throne of Zeus, at the palace of the immortals on Mount Olympos. Zeus hadn't invited them to visit and was a little startled to see them, but he decided to be polite. They were his nephews, after all, since Poseidon was his brother, and so he ordered food and drink to be served. The Olympians gathered at the table but soon lost their appetites when Ephialtes wolfed down an entire cow. Otos, who wasn't quite so hungry, was satisfied with a whole pig. The two giants consumed whole loaves of bread and pitcher after pitcher of wine.

When they were finally satisfied, Zeus asked the brothers, "To what do I owe the, er, pleasure of this visit?"

Ephialtes belched and Otos wiped his greasy hands on a passing sheep. "We need wives," he said.

Zeus was confused. "And what can I do to help you with that?"

Ephialtes leaned back and pointed at Zeus's wife, Hera, who couldn't hide her disgust. "I want *her.*" Hera's disgust instantly turned to fury.

"And I'll take this one." Otos grabbed the goddess of the moon, Artemis, who had grown bored and was trying to sneak away to go on a hunt. She twisted out of his grasp and stood fuming behind her father.

"Now, boys," Zeus protested, "this isn't funny. Come, tell me what you really want. Name any girl on earth—or any nymph—and I'll see that she's yours."

"I want *her,*" Ephialtes repeated, leering at the queen of the gods, and Otos said, "And I said I'll take that feisty one." Artemis eluded his grasp this time.

Zeus rose from his throne and thundered, "THIS IS OUTRAGEOUS!" He flung his arm at the Aloadae, and lightning crackled from his fingertips.

The brothers tumbled down the slopes of Mount Olympos. But faster than seemed possible for such enormous beings, they were soon on their feet again and racing up the mountain.

"Quick!" Hermes shouted, flapping the wings on his sandals. He shot up into the air, followed hastily by the rest of the gods. They settled onto a cloud and watched as Ephialtes and Otos roared in frustration, leaping up to grab at the feet that the gods dangled just out of their reach.

"They'll get bored and go home soon," Hestia, the goddess of the hearth, said reassuringly. The gods settled down to wait.

Sure enough, it wasn't long before the huge brothers went trotting down the mountain. The relieved gods were preparing to go back home when, to their dismay, they saw that the Aloadae had reappeared, carrying something enormous between them. Apollo leaned dangerously far over the edge of the cloud to see what it was. When he sat up again, he appeared perplexed.

"They're bringing another mountain," he said. The gods peered down and saw the brothers drop the mountain on top of Mount Olympos, which brought the new mountain's peak alarmingly close to them.

A bewildered-looking shepherd and a flock of sheep that had been grazing on the topmost slope of the newly-arrived mountain stared up at the gods. "I would get out of there if I were you," the wise goddess Athena advised him. The man scampered down the hill, driving his flock in front of him. He was just in time, for an instant later, a third mountain landed right where he had been standing. Now the Aloadae were almost within reach of the cloud where the gods were huddled.

"What are we going to do now?" little Ganymede, the cupbearer of the gods, asked anxiously.

"I'm not going to put up with this!" the war god, Ares, shouted, and he flew at the brothers, his sword drawn. But Ephialtes grabbed him. He stuffed the furious god into an empty wine jar and put a stopper in its mouth. He and Otos laughed until they cried at the muffled shouts of "Let me out of here!" that came from the jar.

At last, the Aloadae became bored with their attempt to reach the gods. But they didn't go home. For the next thirteen months, they lay around on the mountain, grabbing and roasting sheep from passing flocks, stealing wine from farmers, and in general making a nuisance of themselves. Meanwhile, Ares shouted and pounded in the wine jar, and the rest of the gods remained trapped on the cloud.

When Artemis couldn't stand it anymore, she dropped two of her spears, accidentally on purpose, off the cloud. When the brothers picked them up with glee, she flew down, making sure they didn't see her. She landed behind a bush and turned herself into a deer.

"Be careful, daughter," Zeus breathed from his perch in the clouds. He had no idea what she was planning, but *something* had to be done.

Her small hooves making scarcely any noise, Artemis came out from behind the bush. Then she deliberately stepped on a twig, which cracked loudly enough to catch the attention of the Aloadae. She approached the brothers on her slender deer legs, her huge brown eyes watching them as they fumbled with the spears she had dropped, which looked like tiny toys in their enormous hands.

Suddenly, she ran between them. Simultaneously, the brothers shouted, "I've got her!" and hurled their weapons just at the moment that Artemis made a mighty leap to safety. Ephialtes's spear landed in Otos's chest, and Otos's spear pierced Ephialtes's, and both of them dropped dead.

Artemis turned herself back into her normal form and freed Ares. He didn't even stop to thank her, just went screaming out and up into the heavens, shaking his bow and arrows in fury that his tormentors had died before he'd had a chance to take his revenge.

The Aloadae didn't escape punishment, however. I saw them when I was in the realm of the dead, and they're miserable. They're spending eternity tied back-to-back to a column, on top of which sits a screech owl that makes so much noise, day and night, that the brothers never find peace.

LUCKY THIRTEEN

Most of the Western world counts twelve months in a year, but there are actually thirteen moon cycles in 365 days. Saying that Ares was held captive for thirteen months, then, means that he was imprisoned for a year.

MAYBE THEY WEREN'T *ALL* BAD

Oddly enough for such bad-mannered guys, the Aloadae were credited with founding some cities and even with bringing civilization to humanity.

THIS IS THE END

Just one more to go! It's about time, too. See how low the sun is? If I don't tell you another story you haven't heard in the next few minutes, I'll lose all chance of seeing Eurydice again. I'll be stuck here, just another rock in another forest somewhere in the world, and the water running down my front really will be my tears.

Okay, honestly? They've been tears the whole time. I just said they were condensation because nowadays some people think it's a sign of weakness for a man to cry. I prefer my own time, when manly tears were nothing to be ashamed of.

Anyway, if I fail, at least I won't need to tell stories anymore, which I guess will be a relief. Maybe I'll wait until people come by and yell "Boo!" just to see them jump. But I'd rather be released from this rock and go back to the realm of the dead, for good this time, and be with my dear Eurydice forever.

Let's see, one more. What shall I tell you about? I'm all talked out. This is really the end.

What do you mean, I should tell you about that? About what? Oh, about the end! I see—I started off by telling you how the world and everything else came into being. So you think I should finish by telling you how humans will come to an end, according to the Greeks? Have you heard that one?

Notice I didn't say "how the world will come to an end" but "how *humans* will come to an end." That's because we Greeks thought that the world itself is eternal. Humanity is another matter. The poet Hesiod, the first person anyone knows of who wrote down the myths in Greece, talked about the "progression" of mankind in his book *Works and Days*.

According to Hesiod, the gods created the first humans, the "golden race," with their own hands. The gods loved their creation, and the first people loved the gods. This golden-age generation lived surrounded by fruits and vegetables, and the people watched over plentiful flocks. They never suffered from illness, and death came to them peacefully at the end of a long, happy life. Eventually, all the golden-age people died, but their spirits remain on earth to watch over humanity.

But the gods were unhappy, since no one was left alive to worship them. So they tried creating humans again. The resulting "silver race" wasn't quite as successful as their first attempt. Each of its members spent one hundred years as a foolish child and died soon after reaching adulthood. Worst of all, the silver-age people neglected the gods, so Zeus destroyed them. They became the gloomy spirits of the underworld.

The next try was an utter disaster. Zeus worked alone this time, but he didn't do very well. The new people, the "bronze race," were arrogant, hard-hearted, and violent. The gods didn't have to bother to destroy them, because they killed one another. Their spirits went to the deepest part of the underworld. I think I saw some of them there, but they weren't the kind of people I felt like hanging around with, so I didn't stay long enough to make sure.

Race number four worked out better. The people that Zeus created in his second solo attempt were the ones we know from mythology: the heroes and demi-gods who did magnificent deeds and founded great cities. Unfortunately, they also tended to kill one another in dreadful wars. The members of the heroic race who survived are still alive today, Hesiod says, but they live far away from us, at the ends of the earth. They dwell on the shore of Okeanos, the eternal ocean that existed even before the gods came into being, where the fields and trees bear fruit in three separate springs every year. Remember Okeanos, from the first story I told you?

When the heroic race turned out to be a bust, Zeus ordered a fifth generation to be made, and that's us. We, according to Hesiod, are the "race of iron." We work hard, and many of us suffer. Still, we have some good things in our lives to keep us happy. But, Hesiod warns, things will get really bad. Babies will already be old when they're born. Parents and children will fight with one another, the laws of hospitality will be forgotten, evildoers will be praised, and envy, "with a scowling face," will go among humans.

At that point, the spirits who make up human conscience, Aidos ("shame over bad behavior") and Nemesis ("righteous indignation"), will give up on mankind and depart from the earth to join the gods. Society will fall apart, and all that will remain to people is sorrow.

Hesiod doesn't say how—or even if—our generation of iron will end or whether another one will come after us. Instead, he follows his chapter on the ages of man with a short fable. It's about a hawk that has seized a nightingale in its talons and scolds it when it cries out. The hawk says, "It's up to me whether to eat you or to let you go. It's stupid to try to fight against someone stronger than you, because you're not going to win. You'll just get hurt worse and will make a fool of yourself. So you might as well shut up and at least keep your dignity, and maybe I'll take pity on you and let you go." Perhaps the poet is telling us there's a glimmer of hope that the iron race won't be destroyed, as long as we don't complain and carry on as best we can.

Did I do it? Did I miscount? Was that seventeen?

I think I did it! Or we did it. You and me. I can't wait to tell everyone how a human kid happened to wander through the woods at just the right time. You saved my life, you know that? Well, not really my life. Rocks aren't alive. Listen to me—I'm so nervous, I'm babbling!

There goes the sun. There's just a tiny little sliver of red left! Surely the gods wouldn't be so cruel as to make me tell all those stories and then not reward me. Oh, no! It's almost gone!

Wait—who is that coming toward me? Do you see her? She looks the way I remember her, but I haven't seen her for three thousand years, so I can't be sure. Ah! The light of the setting sun is shining on her face! She's smiling and waving, and it looks like—is it—could it be—Eury—

The talking rock falls silent, and as the last rays of the sun strike it, you see that it is now just an ordinary stone, lying quietly next to a stream, with nothing special to set it apart from any other stone. Somehow you know that you won't hear any more stories from this gray lump, down the front of which run two deep clefts where moss has gathered. The moss is still damp, but water no longer runs through the channels.

Stand near the rock, though, and wait until the birds and squirrels have fallen silent and the night creatures have not yet begun to stir. In those few moments of stillness, listen closely. If you're lucky, you'll hear the merry sounds of a lyre and flute playing a wedding song, and you'll hear the laughter of the newlyweds and the cheers and congratulations of the guests.

If you're fortunate enough to hear the party for the wedding of Orpheus and Eurydice, walk away quietly and don't disturb them. They've waited three thousand years to be together, after all, and they deserve their celebration.

APPENDIX A
A NOTE ABOUT SPELLING

English-speaking fans of Greek myths are familiar with some Greek names and words such as Hercules, siren, and centaur. But these are English versions of the Latin spelling of Greek names, and they're different from the Greek originals.

The Greek and Latin alphabets were similar—in fact, the Greek alphabet was the ancestor of the Latin alphabet—but there are some differences between them. For instance, Greek used the letter "κ" (kappa). Latin didn't have a "k," but that didn't matter, since for most of their history, Romans pronounced the letter "c" like "k." This means that the Romans could use a "c" where Greek had a kappa. For example, the Romans wrote the Greek κένταυρος (kentauros) as *centaurus*. (Words that end in –os [-ος] in ancient Greek usually end in –us in Latin.)

The Latin language lacked some of the sounds in the Greek language, so the Romans left out some important Greek letters (φ and ψ, for example), since they didn't need them for Latin words. When the Romans wrote Greek words, they used "ph" and "ps" to represent the sounds made by φ and ψ.

At first, the Romans left three more Greek letters out of their alphabet, because they thought they would never need them. Later, when they changed their minds, they tacked these three letters ("x" [ξ], "y" [υ], and "z" [ζ]) onto the end of their alphabet. Greek had two forms of the letter "e," with slightly different pronunciations (ε and η), and two forms of the letter "o" (o and ω). The Romans ignored the small differences in pronunciation and used "e" for both ε and η (sometimes η became "a"), and "o" for both o and ω. And that's how words with those letters have come into English.

The Romans who retold and wrote down Latin translations of Greek writings did the best they could with the spelling of Greek names—sometimes changing only a letter or two, sometimes more. English speakers, who usually read the Roman versions of Greek myths, generally adopted a variation of the Roman spelling. One thing they did was to lop the ending off most Greek nouns, whether they came through Latin or straight from Greek. Getting back to κένταυρος (kentauros), then, we have κένταυρος (Greek) → centaurus (Latin) → centaur (English).

In this book, you'll see the standard English spelling (the one based on Latin) for people, gods, and place names if the more Greek-like version would be difficult for someone already familiar with Greek myths to recognize. The Greek version—or at least as close as you can get with the Latin alphabet—is used in all other cases.

UPPER CASE	LOWER CASE	NAME	ENGLISH
Α	α	alpha	A
Β	ß	beta	B
Γ	γ	gamma	G
Δ	δ	delta	D
Ε	ε	epsilon	E
Ζ	ζ	zeta	Z
Η	η	eta	E
Θ	θ	theta	TH
Ι	ι	iota	I
Κ	κ	kappa	K
Λ	λ	lambda	L
Μ	μ	mu	M
Ν	ν	nu	N
Ξ	ξ	xi	X
Ο	ο	omicron	O
Π	π	pi	P
Ρ	ρ	rho	R
Σ	σ, ς	sigma	S
Τ	τ	tau	T
Υ	υ	upsilon	U, Y
Φ	φ	phi	PH
Χ	χ	chi	CH, KH
Ψ	ψ	psi	PS
Ω	ω	omega	O

What is the modern English equivalent of these ancient Greek names? (Ignore the accent marks above the letters!)

Ἀθηνά

Εὐρυδίκη

Κύκλωψ

Ὀρφεύς

APPENDIX B
A NOTE ABOUT PRONUNCIATION

Today nobody can be sure exactly how ancient Greek was pronounced, although linguists (people who study language) have some good ideas about it. Most English-speakers don't try to pronounce all of the names of ancient Greek people, animals, and gods the way linguists think the Greeks did, but have come up with their own pronunciations for the most common ones of them. There can be several options for pronouncing some of the names, and often people in one English-speaking country will say them differently from people in another English-speaking country. Most people in Britain, for example, call the half-man, half-bull monster the "MY-nuh-tor," whereas most people in the United States say "MIN-uh-tor."

The list below shows how a lot of English speakers would expect to hear some of the Greek words used in this book pronounced. If a name isn't on this list, pronounce "ch" like "k" and "ph" like "f," say most "e's" at or near the end of a word like "ee", usually pronounce "a" like the "a" in "hat," and the "o" to rhyme with "toe" except in the endings "-os" and "-on," which roughly rhyme with "boss" and "on," and you're on the right track.

PEOPLE, DEITIES, ANIMALS

Agamemnon: a-ga-MEM-non

Aphrodite: a-fro-DI-tee

Apollo: a-PAH-lo

Arachne: a-RAK-nee

Ares: AIR-ees

Artemis: AR-tem-is

Cerberus: SER-ber-us

Chiron: KI-ron

Dionysos: di-oh-NI-sus

Epimetheus: e-pi-MEE-thee-us

Eros: EH-ros

Europa: yoo-RO-pa

Gaia: GEE-a or GUY-a

Ganymede: GA-nuh-meed

Hades: HAY-deez

Medea: mu-DEE-a

Minos: MEE-nos or MY-nos

Odysseus: oh-DISS-ee-us

Orpheus: OR-fee-us

Persephone: per-SEF-uh-nee

Poseidon: puh-SI-dun

Priam: PRI-am

Prometheus: pro-MEE-thee-us

Theseus: THEE-zee-us

Zeus: ZOOS

PLACES

Delos: DEE-los or DEH-los

Mycenae: my-SEE-nee

Nemea: nuh-MEE-a

NYMPHS, MONSTERS, ETC.

dryad: DRI-ad

Minotaur: MIN-uh-tor or MY-nuh-tor

naiad: NI-ad

GLOSSARY

(Names and words marked with an asterisk are
identified elsewhere in the glossary)

IMMORTALS: TITANS

The Titans were a race of gods who came before (and often were the parents of) the more familiar Olympian gods. Despite the importance of the Titans, no Greek temples are dedicated to them and there's no record of any festivals in their honor. As soon as worship of the Olympians became common, the Titans pretty much dropped out of sight, only occasionally entering into a myth. These are the Titans who are mentioned in this book:

Eos (Ἠώς or Ἔως; Roman Aurora): the goddess who brought the dawn to the earth each day. The dew sometimes found on grass in the morning was said to be made of her tears. Some think that her name is related to the English word *Easter*, because Easter comes in the spring, which is the dawn of the year.

Epimetheus (Ἐπιμηθεύς; see Prometheus)

Gaia (Γαῖα) or **Ge** (Γῆ; Roman Terra): the goddess of the earth, as well as the earth itself. She and her husband

Uranus, who was both the sky god and the sky, must have had a lively household, since among their children were most of the rest of the Titans, the Cyclopes (savage one-eyed giants), Thunder, Lightning, and three sons who had one hundred arms and fifty heads each.

Okeanos (Ὠκεανός): the primordial ocean and the god who represented it. Sometimes this ocean is pictured as encircling the part of the earth that, as far as the Greeks knew, was inhabited. Later, the Greeks imagined that Okeanos was like a belt around the earth's equator. If you think the Greeks believed the world was flat, it might surprise you to learn that they knew about the equator. Actually, starting in the sixth century BCE, some Greeks thought that the earth was probably round. By the third century BCE, Greek astronomers had confirmed this theory and even estimated pretty accurately how big our planet is.

Prometheus (Προμηθεύς): a Titan who stole fire from the forge of Hephaistos* to give to humans, whom he had created out of clay. His brother Epimetheus created animals. Early Greek writers thought that "Prometheus" meant "forethinker" and "Epimetheus" meant "afterthinker." But many modern scholars think that "Prometheus" comes from a word meaning "thief," and that the character of Epimetheus was made up by the poet Hesiod.

IMMORTALS: GODS AND GODDESSES

These deities are often referred to as Olympian gods, because they lived on top of Mount Olympos, in Greece. These are some of the Olympians mentioned in this book. There are many more.

Aphrodite (Ἀφροδίτη; Roman Venus): the goddess of love. Her father was either Uranus (the sky) or Zeus*. In the myth that says her father is Uranus, there's no mother involved; Aphrodite is born out of the sea. In the myth where

Zeus is her father, her mother is a Titan* named Dione. Curiously, "Dione" (Διώνη) is the feminine form of "Zeus" (in the way that Charlotte is the feminine form of Charles, and Andrea is the feminine form of Andrew). In that sense, this myth may be saying that Zeus/Dione was Aphrodite's father *and* her mother, so no matter which myth you follow, the goddess of love is the daughter of Zeus only. She was married to Hephaistos*.

Apollo (Ἀπόλλων; Roman Apollo or Phoebus): the god of the sun (well, one of them), music, and poetry. Apollo had a lot of other duties, too. Among them were welcoming boys into manhood, bringing plagues on people, and speaking through specially chosen women to deliver prophecies. One of Apollo's epithets (a kind of nickname or second, descriptive name) is "Smintheus" (Σμινθεύς), which means either "from the town of Sminthos" or something to do with mice (ancient Greek for "mouse" is *sminthos*, or σμίνθος). If it's the mice, does this mean that Apollo was the mouse god? The mouse exterminator? Something to do with mice as carriers of plague? Nobody knows. His father was Zeus* and his mother was a Titan*; his twin sister was Artemis*.

Ares (Ἄρης; Roman Mars): the god of destructive war. He was ferocious and bloodthirsty. His parents were Zeus* and Hera*. His own father hated him, and even though he was the god of war, he didn't always win his battles. In the Trojan War, he was on the losing (Trojan) side.

Artemis (Ἄρτεμις; Roman Diana): the goddess of the moon and the hunt, and the queen of the nymphs. Her father was Zeus* and her mother was a Titan*; her twin brother was Apollo*. She took a vow never to marry. She watched over the various stages of a woman's life, welcoming her into adulthood and taking care of her in childbirth. She was such an expert in childbirth that when she was just a few minutes old, she acted as a midwife to help her mother give birth to Apollo.

Eros (Ἔρως; Roman Cupid): the god of love. The earliest myths say that he was born before any other deity, including Eurynome and Okeanos (see "The Big Bang," page TK). Later, some said that Eros was the son of Aphrodite*, or else that he was born from the sea along with her. Anyone he shot with a golden arrow would fall in love with the next person she or he saw. But he also had arrows made of lead, and those caused hatred instead.

Hephaistos (Ἥφαιστος; Roman Vulcan): the god of every craft that has to do with hot metal (blacksmithing, sculpting, metal casting, etc.). He made lightning, as well as the gods' thrones and armor. He created robots to do some of his work for him; these included three-legged pots called tripods that walked to Mount Olympos* and back to the forge again. His parents were Zeus* and Hera,* or maybe just Hera. He was born with a shriveled leg or broke a leg when one of his parents tossed him off Mount Olympos—either way, he walked with a limp. He was married (unhappily) to Aphrodite*.

Hera (Ἥρα; Roman Juno): the queen of the gods. She watched over women, particularly at their weddings, and women called upon her for help during childbirth. She had many epithets (see entry for Apollo* for a definition) that show she was in charge of every stage of a girl/woman's life: She was called Pais (Παῖς), Child; Parthenos (Παρθένος), Maiden; Teleia (Τελεία), Perfected (= married); and Chere (Χήρη), Widowed. (In ancient Greece, women were strictly controlled by men, and their marital status determined how they were treated. That's why Hera's epithets mostly have to do with marital status.) Early Greeks worshipped their deities not in temples but in the open air. One of the first—maybe *the* first—roofed temple in Greece was dedicated to Hera, which shows how important she was. She was married to Zeus*.

Herakles (Ἡρακλὲης; Roman Hercules): the greatest Greek hero. He became immortal right before he would otherwise have died. He was very strong, hot-tempered, a loyal friend, and, unfortunately, subject to fits of insanity. His parents were Zeus* and a woman named Alkmene; his twin brother had a mortal father. His name means "Glory of Hera*," which has puzzled people since ancient times, since Hera hated him. In fact, as soon as he was born, Hera sent two snakes to kill him in his cradle, but he strangled them. Some think that since his mother's name, Alkmene, means "strong in anger," this might not have been a name but an epithet (see entry for Apollo for a definition) for Hera. This would mean that Hera was his mother, which would explain the name but still wouldn't explain the snakes.

Hermes (Ἑρμὴς; Roman Mercury): the protector of herdsmen, and the god of merchants and prosperity. He was skilled in both debate and trickery. A young boys' festival, in which many sports were played and contests of strength, speed, and agility took place, was called the Hermeia in his honor. Because of this, he is the god of the gymnasium. Hermes conducted souls to the afterlife and occasionally served as messenger of the gods (although Iris, goddess of the rainbow, normally performed this task). He is usually shown wearing a winged hat and winged sandals. He was the great-grandfather of Odysseus*, the hero of Homer's *Odyssey*.

Persephone (Περσεφόνη; Roman Proserpina): the queen of the underworld. She ruled there half the year and lived on earth during the other half. She was the daughter of the goddess of the harvest. Also known as Kore (the Maiden), she was kidnapped by Hades, god of the underworld, as she was picking flowers. She is known by many other names: Persephassa (Περσεφάσσα), Persephatta (Περσεφάττα), Pherepapha (Φερέπαφα), Periphona (Πηριφόνα), Pherephatta (Φερεφάττα), and Phersephassa (Φερσέφασσα).

Those names don't look Greek, which makes some scholars think Persephone's origins weren't Greek and that the Greeks had difficulty pronouncing her name, so they came up with all those variations.

Poseidon (Ποσειδῶν; Roman Neptune): the god of the sea, earthquakes, and horses. He and his two brothers (Zeus*, the sky god, and Hades, who ruled the underworld) governed the earth. Poseidon had strange taste in women. His wife was a sea creature, and his girlfriends included one of the Erinyes—the "avengers" of the underworld, who wore snakes around their waists and whose eyes dripped blood—and Medusa, the Gorgon who had snakes for hair (although she and Poseidon got together before her hair turned serpentine).

Zeus (Ζεύς; Roman Jupiter or Jove): the king of the gods. He was born on the island of Crete and hidden there from his father, who wanted to eat him. He was raised by either Gaia*, a nymph, a goat, or a shepherd family. He was married to Hera* and/or to a nymph or Titan* named Dione (see Aphrodite*). He had dozens of children.

OTHER MYTHOLOGICAL FIGURES

Argonauts (Ἀργοναύται; see Jason*)

Chiron (Χείρων): a centaur (half man, half horse) who was noted for his wisdom, unlike other centaurs, who were wild and crazy. His father was the leader of the Titans* and his mother was a nymph. (The wild centaurs were descended from a raincloud.) After Herakles* accidentally wounded him with a poisoned arrow, Chiron was in such agony that he wanted to die, but he couldn't, because he was immortal. He volunteered to die in place of Prometheus*, who was being punished by the gods for stealing fire from them to help the humans he had created. Zeus* granted Chiron's wish and placed him in the heavens as the constellation Sagittarius.

Europa (Ευρώπη): a princess whose name means "wide face." (She was probably originally a cow goddess, not a human; cows have wide faces.) As a human, Europa and her friends were picking flowers one day when she saw a beautiful white bull, and for some reason, she climbed on its back. The bull turned out to be Zeus*, and he swam across the sea to Crete with her riding atop him. Zeus gave Europa three gifts: a huge robot named Talos (see "The Bronze Man of Crete," p. TK), a magical hound named Lailaps (see "But Does She *Really* Love You?", p. TK, and "The Hurricane Hound and the Teumessian Fox," p. TK), and a spear that never missed its target (see the myths with Lailaps).

Fates (Μοῖραι [The Ones Who Divide Things Up]): immortal women who decide how long individual people will live, whether they will be happy or unhappy, etc. Their parents were Night and Violent Death (who were also the parents of Doom, Death, and other unpleasant things), and they were born before the gods or even the Titans*. They spin, measure, and cut thread to determine a person's fate.

The ancient Greeks believed that knots tied in string could cast a spell. String was sometimes used in communication and recordkeeping as well.

Ganymede (Γανυμήδης): a prince of Troy* who was so handsome that Zeus* turned himself into an eagle and snatched him up to Mount Olympos to serve as his cupbearer. Zeus gave Ganymede's father a pair of horses to repay him for the loss of his son.

Helen of Troy (Ἑλένη): the stepdaughter of one king and wife of another (Menelaos of Sparta). Her father was Zeus* and her mother was either a princess named Leda, or Nemesis, the spirit of retribution (which more or less means "payback"). She went to Troy* with the Trojan Prince

Paris*. Some myths say he kidnapped her; others say she ran away with him. When Menelaos and other kings from Greece attacked Troy to get her back, it started the Trojan War.

If Helen didn't go with Paris of her own free will, it was the second time she was kidnapped. The first time, a "hero" named Theseus stole her from her home when she was just a child, and her brothers rescued her.

Jason (Ἰάσων): the son of a king. Jason's half-brother, or maybe his cousin, massacred the rest of their family. Jason became the captain of a ship called the *Argo*. He and sailors called the Argonauts* went to the land of Kolkhis and stole the Golden Fleece with the help of the Kolkhian princess and priestess Medea*. According to some accounts, he later told her he was going to marry someone else, and Medea took a brutal vengeance on him. Others say they ruled together peacefully for years.

Medea (Μήδεια): daughter of a king, niece of a sorceress, granddaughter of the sun god. Medea was a priestess, probably of the sun god in the form of a ram. She helped the hero Jason* steal the ram's fleece, which was sacred to her people, the Kolkhians. Either she or Jason killed her brother during their escape. After she and Jason separated, she married the king of Athens.

Minos (Μίνως): a son of Zeus* and Europa*. According to the Greeks, he was the king of Crete and the stepfather of the half-man, half-bull Minotaur. Probably, though, "minos" isn't a name but a Cretan title meaning "king" or "war chief," and the Minotaur was actually a priest (fully human) who wore a bull's-head mask during ceremonies.

Odysseus (Ὀδυσσεύς, also known as Oulixeus [Οὐλιξεύς] or Oulixes [Οὐλίξης]; Latin Ulysses or Ulixes): a king whose return from the Trojan War was delayed ten years. The story of his invention of the Trojan Horse is told in Homer's

Iliad, and his trip home is recounted in the *Odyssey*. Descended from the trickster god Hermes*, Odysseus was a master liar. His wife was a first cousin of Helen of Troy*.

Orpheus (Ὀρφεύς): a mythical singer, lyre player, poet, and prophet. The Greeks said he founded a religion called the Orphic Mysteries. Not much is known about this religion except that its followers believed that when people died, they were reborn in another (human) body.

Pandora (Πανδώρα): the first woman, whose name means "all-gifted," "all-giving," or "all gifts." She opened a jar—not a box—that contained the ills that have plagued humans ever since, leaving only Hope inside to ease humanity's pains. There's a problem with that story: How is it that leaving Hope locked up in the jar enables it to *help* people? Wouldn't Hope have to be released in order to have any effect, the way the ills had to be released to cause harm? An ancient writer named Theognis evidently thought so. He said the jar actually contained only *good* things, and that once they were released, they flew away, never to confer their blessings on humans. Since Hope is still in the jar, it's still available.

Paris (Πάρις): a prince of Troy* who had at least sixty-seven brothers and eighteen sisters (some writers say even more). He chose Aphrodite* as the winner in a goddess beauty contest, because she promised to give him the most beautiful woman in the world if he did so. This led to the Trojan War. Paris was a very good archer, but he didn't behave bravely during the war; he mostly avoided combat. He did challenge Helen's husband, King Menelaos, to a duel, but he fought so badly that he was on the point of being killed when Aphrodite, grateful that Paris had named her the most beautiful of the goddesses, swooped down and carried him to safety.

PLACES

Argos (Ἄργος): a city about halfway between the power-house city-states of Athens* and Sparta*. Argos has been continuously inhabited for about 7,000 years.

Athens (ancient Greek Ἀθῆναι [Athenai]): the capital of modern Greece, and one of the most important cities—some would say *the* most important—of ancient Greece. The site of Athens has been continuously inhabited for more than 7,000 years. When people talk about "ancient Greece" and "ancient Greeks," they often are really referring to Athens and the Athenians.

Crete (Κρήτη): the fifth-largest island in the Mediterranean Sea, and the largest Greek island. Crete was first settled about 130,000 years ago and was later the home of the advanced Minoan civilization.

Mount Ida (Ἴδη): Two sacred mountains, one on Crete* and the other in western Turkey, are called Ida. Zeus* was left on the Mount Ida in Crete to keep him safe from his murderous father. Zeus kidnapped Ganymede* off the Mount Ida in Turkey, which is also where Paris* met his wife (see "An Oread Scorned," p. TK).

Mount Olympos (Ὄλυμπος): the highest mountain in Greece and one of the highest in Europe, home of the major Greek gods. Some ancient writers say that the gods lived in a bronze dome *above* the mountain, not on the mountain itself.

Mycenae (Μυκήνη or Μυκῆναι): Before Athens* and Sparta* rose in importance, Mycenae was one of the most powerful city-states in ancient Greece. The period from about 1600-1100 BCE is called "Mycenaean" today. The origin of the name is unknown and probably isn't Greek, but the Greeks used the word and tried to figure out what it meant. The closest Greek word they could find was "myces" (μύκης), meaning "mushroom." To explain why that word would become the name of a great city-state, they came up with a pretty feeble story about Mycenae's founder picking a mushroom there.

oracle: both the place where a god spoke through a person and the person who did the speaking. If that person was a woman, she might also be called a sibyl. The most famous of these women were the Cumaean Sibyl, who lived in southern Italy (then part of the Greek world), and the Pythia, who spoke words inspired by Apollo* at his temple in the Greek city of Delphi.

Sparta (Σπάρτη): a powerful city on the Peloponnesus, the squarish peninsula that makes up southwestern mainland Greece. Sparta concentrated most of its resources in its military. Paradoxically, Sparta was one of the few places in the ancient world in which girls were treated almost as well as boys, since the Spartans recognized that in order to give birth to and raise strong sons, women have to be strong and healthy.

Troy (Τροία [Troia], Ἴλιον [Ilion], or Ἴλιος [Ilios]): a city in what is now Turkey. The famous poem the *Iliad*, by Homer, is about a war between the Greeks (led by King Menelaos of Mycenae*) and the Trojans (led by King Priam of Troy and his sons). No one knows if there ever was such a war or if Homer made it up, basing his tale on battles between Greeks and Trojans, probably over control of trade.

ACKNOWLEDGMENTS

Many thanks to Lara Perkins, without whose expert guidance and encouragement I never would have attempted this project. Thanks also to Barbara Tsakirgis of the Departments of Classical Studies and Art History at Vanderbilt University, who read an early draft of this manuscript and corrected errors; any that have crept in since that reading are my responsibility. And as always, my love and thanks to Greg.

ABOUT THE AUTHOR

Tracy Barrett has loved Greek mythology ever since she first read *D'Aulaire's Book of Greek Myths*. In college she majored in Classics with a specialty in ancient Greek art and architecture, and she has made many trips to Italy, Greece, North Africa, and Turkey to visit museums and ancient ruins. Five of her more than twenty books relate to the ancient Classical world: *Dark of the Moon* (a retelling of the myth of the Minotaur), *King of Ithaka* (Homer's *Odyssey* as seen by Odysseus's son, Telemachos), the time-travel novel *On Etruscan Time*, the nonfiction *The Ancient Greek World* (co-authored with Jennifer Roberts), and now *The Song of Orpheus*.

She lives in Nashville, Tennessee (the home of the world's most complete full-scale replica of the Parthenon) with her husband and her dog, Pericles.

CPSIA information can be obtained
at www.ICGtesting.com
Printed in the USA
LVOW04s2300010816
498607LV00015BA/765/P